MURDER AT
LE BIJOU BISTRO

A Northwest Cozy Mystery - Book 5

BY

DIANNE HARMAN

Published by: Dianne Harman
www.dianneharman.com

Interior, cover design and website by
Vivek Rajan

ISBN: 978-1983584916

CONTENTS

Acknowledgments

Prologue

1   Chapter One   1

2   Chapter Two   7

3   Chapter Three   14

4   Chapter Four   21

5   Chapter Five   26

6   Chapter Six   33

7   Chapter Seven   42

8   Chapter Eight   48

9   Chapter Nine   55

10   Chapter Ten   63

11   Chapter Eleven   71

12   Chapter Twelve   79

13   Chapter Thirteen   87

14   Chapter Fourteen   94

15   Chapter Fifteen   101

16   Chapter Sixteen   106

17   Chapter Seventeen   112

18   Chapter Eighteen   121

19	Epilogue	130
20	Recipes	134
21	About Dianne	140
22	Surprise!	142

ACKNOWLEDGMENTS

To my family, who unfailingly tell me no matter what occurs in my life that "it should be in one of your books" – such as recently getting stuck in one of the wildfires that were sweeping through California - thank you!

To Tom, who is always there with thoughts, ideas, and changes that make my books ever so much better, to say nothing of taking over the Harman household duties - thank you!

To Vivek, who continues to give me good advice, design amazing covers for my books, and do all the computer things that are beyond me - thank you!

And to the countless unnamed and unknown people I see and meet, who through their mannerisms, idle conversations, and casual remarks, provide the basis for the characters, plots, and dialogue found in my books - thank you!

And to all of you who take the time to buy, borrow, read, or review my books, I appreciate it more than you'll ever know - thank you!

Win FREE Paperbacks every week!

Go to www.dianneharman.com/freepaperback.html and get your FREE copies of Dianne's books and favorite recipes immediately by signing up for her newsletter.

Once you've signed up for her newsletter you're eligible to win three paperbacks. One lucky winner is picked every week. Hurry before the offer ends!

PROLOGUE

DeeDee Wilson chewed on her lower lip as the car inched through the early evening downtown Seattle rush hour traffic. She glanced at her wristwatch for the third time in five minutes, but the line of cars was going nowhere.

With a soft sigh, DeeDee glanced over at her boyfriend, Jake Rogers, who was driving. Not that the car was moving. Jake had one hand on the steering wheel, and his other elbow was resting on the edge of the window. He turned to DeeDee and smiled, the bright blue of his eyes illuminated against his tan weathered-looking face.

"Relax, honey," he said, reaching over and squeezing her hand. "We'll be there soon. I know you're excited to see Cassie and Al. Is that a present for the birthday girl?" He nodded at the silver gift-wrapped package on her lap with the contrasting plush black velvet bow on top.

DeeDee nodded. "Yep. I know Cassie said not to, but you know me when it comes to birthdays."

The traffic started moving and Jake pulled his hand away as the car started to creep forward. "I sure do. What did we get her?"

DeeDee chuckled. "You'll have to wait and see. Oh wait, where have I heard that before. Sounds familiar, doesn't it?" DeeDee raised her index finger to her face. Pouting, she tapped her chin.

"If you're referring to your own birthday surprise, I swear all will be revealed soon," Jake said, signaling to turn. "You're like a broken record, going on, and on…" He made a squeaking noise. "And on."

"Better be," DeeDee muttered. "You've been spinning this out for almost three months. My patience is wearing thin. It's not every year a woman turns fifty. Cassie is younger than me, but just by a little. Her big 5-oh is next year."

"What date's your birthday again?" Jake said, scratching his head.

DeeDee looked sideways at Jake and saw his face twitch. "As if you don't know," she scolded. "April 14th. I thought it would be permanently etched in your memory."

"Hmm." Jake smiled. "I'll try to remember." He drummed on the steering wheel with his fingers. "What say we find a parking space and walk the rest of the way to Pioneer Square? The traffic is so slow it will probably be quicker to walk anyway, plus it's a beautiful evening." Without waiting for DeeDee's reply, Jake swerved the car with a sudden jerk, and pulled into a parking garage entrance that opened onto the street.

It was a mild evening, just a pleasant fifteen-minute walk to where they were meeting their dinner companions. DeeDee linked her arm through Jake's and snuggled up close to him.

"Tell me again," Jake asked, "what are Al and Cassie's plans, now that Al's decided he can't bear to be apart from Cassie for more than a few days?"

DeeDee laughed. Her good friend Cassie Roberts, recently widowed, had met Al through DeeDee several months earlier. "I never thought anyone would capture Cassie's heart after Johnny died, but that's before any of us knew Al. He's one in a million. If Cassie's got any sense, and I know she does, she won't let him get away."

"I don't think Al has any intention of letting that happen," Jake mused. "Although, with Al living in the Cayman Islands, and Cassie in Seattle, something's gotta give."

DeeDee paused in front of an upscale boutique and admired the dress on the mannequin in the window. The vibrant floral pattern put her in the mood for spring and things like dining alfresco and sipping wine on the porch outside her small home next to the beach on Bainbridge Island. She made a mental note to come back and try it on. It could be a gift to herself. After all, her birthday was only a couple of weeks away. She didn't know what secret surprise Jake was planning, but she was hoping it included dinner somewhere special. The dress would be perfect.

She turned back to Jake. "I don't think Al's spent much time in the Caymans since he met Cassie. Last I heard, he was staying in a borrowed penthouse here in the city, and Cassie's settled into a suite at The Four Seasons Hotel while she's house-hunting."

Jake steered DeeDee by the elbow across the street. "Is Cassie still the restaurant critic for The Seattle Times?"

DeeDee grinned. "Oh yes, and she's loving it. Her Food Spy column runs twice a week. I think it's brought out a wicked side in Cassie that no one knew she had, including herself. She doesn't pull any punches when it comes to saying what she thinks about a restaurant. She's earned herself a few enemies in the process, but I guess that comes with the territory."

Jake's face lit up. "Maybe we'll get special treatment at the restaurant tonight. Some of those freebie bite-size things, what are they called again?"

"Amuse-bouche," DeeDee said gently. There was nothing phony or contrived about Jake. He always said exactly what he meant, particularly when it came to food. He liked traditional food, although he was willing to be adventurous when it came to eating out, or testing some of DeeDee's recipes that she intended to use in her catering business, Deelish. "It's a way for chefs to express their big ideas in small bites. And yes, it's a high-end French restaurant we're going to, so there's a good chance we'll get one." Her pace quickened at the sight of two familiar figures on the sidewalk ahead of them. "Look. There's Cassie and Al."

DeeDee pointed towards where a tall, burly man was standing on the sidewalk with his arm around the waist of a petite woman who was gazing up at him, gesturing with her hands as she spoke. The couple was outside the doorway of Le Bijou Bistro. The exterior color of the restaurant was a deep red with the lettering on the sign with its name on it written in a traditional pale yellow colored French script. Floor to ceiling windows that looked out onto the street gave people walking by a view of the dark wooden tables and red chairs inside the restaurant.

The man DeeDee pointed out was in his sixties and was leaning down to hear the woman, pulling her close. The look of adoration the couple shared with each other struck DeeDee with an intensity that was almost physical. She glanced at Jake to see if he'd noticed anything, and knew that he'd seen it too. They were witnessing magical chemistry between two of the people they were proud to call friends, Cassie Roberts and Al De Duco.

It was Cassie who caught sight of DeeDee and Jake first, and her makeup-free face broke into a wide smile as they approached. When Cassie opened her arms to greet DeeDee with a hug, DeeDee was surprised to see it wasn't just her friend's smile that was dazzling. A huge sparkler on Cassie's slender ring finger caught the light. DeeDee estimated it was at least ten carats of the clearest, most flawless diamond she'd ever seen. The ring looked vaguely familiar, but she wasn't sure why.

"Is there something you want to tell me?" DeeDee whispered in Cassie's ear as they embraced.

Cassie pulled back and winked. "Ssh. Don't say anything. Al wants to tell you both when we're inside."

DeeDee turned towards Al. He was beaming as he pulled Jake

close and slapped him on the back in a man-hug. They were already talking about the Seahawks and whether they'd be in the Super Bowl next year.

"Hey, you guys," DeeDee said, approaching Al who kissed her on both cheeks, while Jake did the same to Cassie. "Save the sports talk for later. You've got two beautiful ladies here who are ravenous."

"And thirsty," Cassie quipped.

Al jiggled his sunglasses, which he wore everywhere. DeeDee thought he looked a little grayer around the temples than usual, and realized he'd let his hair dye fade. Cassie's influence suited him well. He looked softer, less scary. Although he was now retired, his years in the Mob had given him a hard edge as well as a few visible scars, although anyone who knew him would vouch that he wouldn't harm a fly—unless it crossed him or someone close to him. Then, that fly was dead.

"Lead the way, ladies," Al said as he bowed and extended his arm towards the door of Le Bijou Bistro.

Inside, the interior of the restaurant was as small and elegant as its name indicated, a French word for just that, small and elegant. The aroma of freshly baked bread and French cooking permeated the air, mixed with something else DeeDee couldn't put her finger on, but which was decidedly French. Herbs, but hard to decipher in what combination.

Cassie greeted the *maitre'd*. "Hi, my name is Cassie Roberts," she smiled. Al stood beside her. "I made a reservation for 7:00 p.m."

The *maitre'd* nodded and looked down at his clipboard. "Ah *bien oui*, a table for two, *Madame*?" he said in a thick French accent, nodding to a candlelit table in the corner. "Table 12 is ready for you now."

Al cleared his throat, causing the expression of the *maitre'd* to flicker.

"Um, it was, but I changed the booking yesterday to four of us," Cassie said politely.

"*Pas de probleme.* One moment, *s'il vous plait,*" the *maitre'd* said.

DeeDee watched him as he clicked his fingers in the air. A waiter, wearing a starched white apron down to his knees, appeared as if by magic. The *maitre'd* pointed to a table by the window, and fired instructions to the employee in French.

Al said something in a low voice to Cassie, who spoke up again. "Not by the window, please, could we sit along the wall at the back instead?"

Her request was met with a solemn nod. "*Bien sur, Madame.* Of course, as you wish."

Moments later, their party was seated at the back of the restaurant at a table away from the kitchen.

"Sorry about that," Cassie said, after the waiter had handed them their menus and showed them the chalkboard with the Specials, or *Plat du Jour* as it was called. "My...I mean, Al, never sits by the window, and he rarely sits at the first table we're offered, either." She lowered her voice. "It's a Mob thing, apparently."

Al was watching Cassie with a mixture of admiration and pride. He cleared his throat again, before addressing DeeDee and Jake across the table. "I gotta come right out and tell ya'," he said, his voice cracking with emotion. "My wife thinks it's kinda' funny, my old habits. But it's all fer a good reason, don'tcha think?"

DeeDee's eyes widened, and she almost shrieked with excitement. "You two got MARRIED?"

Cassie nodded as a smile lit up her face and stretched from ear to ear. Al was gripping her hand looking like he was about to burst with joy. DeeDee was so overcome with happiness for them, she choked up.

"I think I'm going to cry," she said in a tearful voice, before leaping up to go around to the other side of the table to hug and kiss both of them. Jake stood and did the same, and by the time DeeDee sat down again her tears were flowing. "Look at me," she sniffed, reaching in her purse for a tissue. "I'm such a cry-baby." Dabbing her eyes and composing herself, she continued, "We want to hear all about it. Tell us everything."

"Thought I'd better make an honest woman of her," Al said, motioning for the waiter and ordering champagne. "We'll take the Bollinger R.D. 1976," he instructed, and the waiter hurried off, certain he'd be rewarded with a good tip at the end of the evening, since the customer had started out by ordering one of the most expensive things listed on the extensive wine list.

"We were in Las Vegas, and I had no idea," Cassie said. "But Al had it all planned, didn't you, darling?"

Al nodded. "We were at the Harry Connick, Jr. show. I'd arranged for Harry to come up and sing at our table for Cassie," he explained.

Cassie took up the story. "When Harry handed the microphone to Al, and Al started singing to me, I started laughing," she said. "And then the music stopped, and Al got down on one knee. He'd even arranged for Liam and Briana to be there in case I said yes. So, I thought I'd better go through with it. Right, honey?" Her face was flushed as she looked over at her husband, who was looking at her with adoring eyes.

"Show me that rock again," DeeDee said, reaching for Cassie's tiny hand. It was only then she noticed the fine platinum diamond encrusted wedding band, nestled in below the larger ring.

Jake let out a low whistle. "You sure know how to put a ring on a lady's hand, Al," he said, as the waiter arrived with the champagne. After they'd made several toasts to the happy couple and the birthday girl, they finally got around to looking at the menus and ordering their meals.

"I don't know about anyone else, but I can't get past the *Plat du Jour*," DeeDee announced, setting her menu down.

"Hmm," Jake said, glancing up at the chalkboard the waiter had put on their table in addition to the menus. "I think I'll have the same thing. Prosciutto and grilled asparagus with mustard, leg of lamb with sausage stuffing, heirloom tomato salad with burrata and candied walnuts? That sounds good to me."

"Don't forget the meringues with vanilla ice cream, chocolate sauce, and toasted almonds for dessert," DeeDee reminded him with a giggle. She felt Jake's hand reach for hers under the table, and his strong fingers wrapped around hers tightly. Sometimes, with Jake, words were not necessary. This was one of those times.

Cassie and Al ordered different choices off the *a la carte* menu. Cassie explained that she was going to be reviewing the meal for her newspaper column.

"Won't the chef know it's you?" DeeDee wondered aloud, having overheard Cassie state earlier that the booking was in her own name.

Cassie shrugged. "Some restaurant critics go incognito, but that's too cloak and dagger for my liking. I'm only filling in part-time at the paper for now, so I don't see the need for a huge amount of secrecy. The way I look at it, if I make a reservation in my own name, it's like tipping the restaurant off that they might be getting reviewed. Then they can't complain if the review is bad. It's not like they didn't get plenty of warning."

Cassie paused while everyone's appetizers were served. "Mm," she sniffed, inhaling the aroma coming from the dish of small shells that were placed in front of her. She wrote something on a small notepad before lifting a tiny fork and fishing out the contents of one of the shells.

Jake squinted across the table. "What's that, Cassie?"

"Stuffed snails," Cassie said, offering her plate to Jake. "Would you like to try one?"

Jake shook his head from side to side as he unsuccessfully tried not to grimace.

"Looks like Jake won't, but I will," DeeDee grinned, taking Cassie up on the offer. The snails were small and chewy, and tasted of garlic breadcrumbs. Washed down with the champagne chosen by Al, she agreed with Cassie that they were delicious. The conversation was comfortable, the fizz was flowing, the food was excellent, and by the time they had finished eating, a couple of hours had passed.

"So, have you two planned where you're going to live?" Jake asked, when the desserts had been cleared and they were waiting for their coffee to be served.

Al and Cassie looked at each other, and DeeDee said, "Please don't tell me you two are moving to the Cayman Islands. Much as we'd love to come and visit, we'd miss you too much. And what about Liam and Briana?"

Cassie's face clouded over momentarily at the mention of her children, before Al spoke up. "Not the Caymans, although we're gonna keep my place there for vacations. We're buying something much closer to Seattle than that."

Jake's forehead crinkled. "So, you're not buying something in Seattle, but somewhere nearby?"

DeeDee interrupted him, almost squealing with delight as she guessed, "Bainbridge Island?"

"Yep," Al confirmed. "We bought Dana D's ol' place. Just gettin' it fixed up with bulletproof windows before we move in. Ya' know how it is."

"Sure," DeeDee said, with a straight face. Al took personal safety very seriously. With his background in the Mafia, he had good reason to. She glanced over at Cassie again, who seemed distracted. DeeDee sensed it was better not to mention anything at the table, but vowed to find out what had caused her friend's discomfort when she'd mentioned her children.

A commotion from across the room made any more talk of Cassie and Al's house remodeling impossible. A young woman appeared to be choking at a table in the corner, and the man dining with her had jumped up behind her. Heaving her gasping body to her feet, he began to perform the Heimlich Maneuver while stunned guests at the neighboring tables watched in silent horror. The woman retched onto the table, and the man released his grip on her diaphragm, only to have her fall flat on the table in a lifeless heap. Glasses smashed and dishes crashed as her body laid on the top of the table, motionless.

Within seconds, Jake and Al were on their feet and rushing over to the table where the woman was. A few short minutes later they returned to the table where Cassie and DeeDee were sitting. Jake shook his head and said, "It doesn't look like she's going to make it."

A hum of confusion had arisen from the other diners, and the sound of a siren from an approaching ambulance was deafening.

Al took a thick wad of bills out of his pocket and dropped them on the table. "Let's get outta here," he barked, as three paramedics burst through the restaurant door and ran over to the table where the woman was.

"Al, that was the table that was supposed to be ours," Cassie said as they walked past the table. Her voice cracked as Al hurriedly ushered her towards the entrance of the restaurant.

DeeDee felt Jake's steadying hand on the small of her back, and she stayed calm as he guided her through the bistro. Outside, she inhaled the cool night air with a deep breath, and looked at Jake questioningly. He shook his head as an indication for her to stay silent.

Cassie, however, was more vocal. "What happened?" she asked with a look of panic on her face. "That woman's dead, isn't she? The woman who was sitting at our table, the table we were supposed to be at, is dead, right?"

Al looked across at Jake, who nodded.

"What happened, Jake?" DeeDee asked quietly.

"She apparently choked on the cake she had for dessert. She wasn't breathing, so I assume she's dead."

Cassie started to sob, and Al pulled her close to his chest.

DeeDee stammered as she forced her next words out. "And we're supposed to think it was a terrible accident, right?" In her recent experience with murder victims, and unfortunately, she'd had a few, that had not been the case. Her words hung in the air.

Al shook his head. "That's not what the waiters were saying on our way out. *Il y a eu un meurtre.* I understand French pretty good, and unless I'm mistaken, that means there's been a murder."

CHAPTER ONE

Shortly after 10:00 a.m., on a spring-like morning in late March, Myles Lambert pulled off his Burberry overcoat and sat down at his usual table by the window at Coffee or Die located in Pioneer Square, just as he did every day. A creature of habit, his daily routine rarely varied. Rising at 8:00 a.m., he ate breakfast alone in his two-bedroom waterfront apartment in downtown Seattle. Myles' day started with a pot of Earl Grey tea, buttered wholegrain toast spread with a thin layer of orange marmalade, and a handful of vitamins.

The English country-casual style of dress that he'd adopted ever since he'd studied Creative Writing at Oxford University in England in his twenties was reflected in his uniform of loose beige corduroy pants and a navy sweater over a button-down shirt. In spring and summer, he swapped the corduroys for chinos and the sweater came off, but never before May 1st. Tan, leather-soled Church's brogues were his footwear of choice.

Myles opened his laptop and booted it up, the blank screen staring back at him. "Thank you, Riley," he said, smiling at the nubile young woman who brought his order. His eyes followed her back to the counter. Riley was just Myles' type, a shapely brunette in her early twenties. Not that Myles ever indulged his sugar daddy fantasies this close to home. On his occasional trips out-of-town where nobody knew him, he found that friendly company from attractive females less than half his age was not hard to come by in the bars he frequented, so long as he flashed some cash.

Myles took a sip of his double espresso and felt the bitter hit of caffeine jolt his brain into life. Next, a sugar rush, courtesy of a raspberry glazed donut. He always had raspberry, and the staff set one aside for him each morning when the delivery truck arrived from the bakery. After he was finished with the donut, he followed a meticulous hand-washing process with a lemon-scented wet-wipe, the type that came in sealed packets and that Myles carried with him everywhere.

It was only when he'd completed this ritual that he was ready to start writing for the day. Flexing his arthritic fingers, he began to type. The words came slowly, because Myles' current work-in-progress was not a labor of love. It was more a means to an end. The chatter of the other patrons in Coffee or Die and the sounds that came from the coffee machines was a suitable soundtrack for Myles' latest work of riveting non-fiction, A Brief History of Food, the Seattle Edition.

It was one of a series of worldwide food guides aimed at tourists that was being pumped out by an international travel publisher. Myles considered there was no one more qualified than him to write it, and he was certain that it would be recognized by those in the know as setting a new literary standard for culinary writing. His plan was to land a publishing contract and use it as a springboard to a successful career of writing fiction.

"Mind if I join you?"

Myles was interrupted by the chair beside him being pulled out and scraped across the wooden floor. A disheveled woman with frizzy blond hair, flushed cheeks, and carrying an extra fifty pounds proceeded to plop herself down beside him. She waved to the man at the counter. "Hey, Rick, my usual, please." Turning back to Myles, the woman laughed. "Don't look so pleased to see me, Myles. You'd think the dog just brought in a bad smell."

"Gloria." Myles faked a tight smile. "You know I hate dogs.

You're not all that bad. Anyway, fancy seeing you here, and what a coincidence."

"Not really," Gloria said, shifting around in her chair. "These rickety seats aren't made for big butts, are they? Only room for one cheek. Excuse me if I fall off."

"Don't let me stop you," Myles muttered. He brightened up a little after Rick handed a latte and two chocolate muffins to Riley so she could deliver then to Gloria, thus allowing Myles a nice view from behind as Riley returned to her station.

Closing his laptop with a snap, Myles watched Gloria cram the first muffin into her mouth in a couple of bites. A forced smile remained on his face as he watched her eat. Regardless of his personal distaste for the woman, she was his boss and a certain etiquette was required from him. From where he was sitting, etiquette wasn't in Gloria's vocabulary. No one would ever guess the unkempt woman who had joined him was none other than Gloria Ekenbach, Lifestyle Editor of The Seattle Times. She cleaned up well for award ceremonies, but the rest of the time she looked like she'd been dragged through a ditch by a hurricane.

Gloria washed down her first muffin with a slurp of latte and then her gaze settled on Myles. "I thought I'd find you here." She nodded at the laptop on the table. "How's the book coming along?"

Myles' eyes narrowed. "Are you checking up on me, Gloria?"

Gloria shrugged and began to peel the paper wrapping off the second muffin. "Not at all. Checking in with you would be closer. We agreed when you took a sabbatical from your Food Critic column at the newspaper that we'd keep in touch."

"Yes, and I've telephoned you each of the last three months just as you asked me to do. Is there a problem?" Myles tried to ignore the chocolate crumbs that were nestled in the crease of Gloria's double chin.

"Not at all," Gloria said with a grin. She leaned across to touch Myles' arm, and he flinched. "Quite the opposite, in fact. I just want to make sure you know you can take as much time off as you need. I know how important this book is to you, and we're all rooting for you at the paper. Do you think another three months is enough?"

"Hmm." Myles rubbed his chin, hoping he looked pensive, but in reality he was stalling for time. He didn't like the turn the conversation was taking. The fact that Gloria had come to seek him out to tell him not to hurry back to work wasn't a good sign. He'd been the food critic at The Seattle Times for thirty-five years, and the lifestyle suited him well. Who wouldn't like dining out every day in the best restaurants in the city, all on an expense account? Myles had also become a minor celebrity on the Seattle foodie scene, and he enjoyed the special attention he received in the restaurants he frequented. He wasn't about to be ousted from that status without a fight.

Gloria jutted her face closer to his. "I don't want you to worry about the newspaper, Myles. We've got it covered."

"Thanks, Gloria," Myles said, shrinking back. *That woman has no concept of personal space,* he thought to himself. "Very kind of you to let me know." He balled his fists under the table to control the anger that was rising within him.

"You're a fine writer, and I know there are other writing projects you want to do once this book's finished." She gave him a knowing look. "This could be your chance to seize the opportunity and really go for it. You could get to the great unfinished novel that's under your bed."

Myles glared at her. How did she know about his unfinished manuscript, the one he'd been working on for twenty years? But he didn't keep it under the bed, it was boxed away in the second bedroom of his apartment. The room was used as an office, since no one ever came to stay.

He tuned back in to Gloria, who obviously loved the sound of her own voice. "Think it over, Myles," she was saying. "The temporary replacement we hired is happy to stay on for a while if you need more time. She seems to like it." Gloria flashed what appeared to Myles to be a triumphant smile.

"I've read a few of her columns," Myles said carefully. Actually he'd read them all, and thought they were amateurish and badly written. "Cassie Roberts, isn't that her name?"

Gloria nodded with enthusiasm. "Yes. I know her style's a lot less polished than yours, but she has a chatty down-to-earth voice the readers can't get enough of. I thought it would take the pressure off of you, knowing that the column's in good hands. So don't feel you have to rush back to work, Myles. Really, there's no rush at all." She beamed at him expectantly. "I hope you're pleased?"

Myles nodded. He could feel the veins pulsing in his neck.

"Excellent." Gloria stood up. "I'm glad that's settled. Call me in July, no, make it August. I don't want to hear from you again until you've typed The End on your novel. Got it?"

"Sure," Myles said, with a heavy dose of sarcasm.

"Oh, and Myles?"

"Yes, Gloria?"

"You're welcome."

Myles watched with disgust as Gloria waddled out of Coffee or Die. Heaving himself out of his chair, he crossed the floor and removed that day's copy of The Seattle Times from the newspaper rack on the wall. Returning to his table, he turned to the Food Spy column and stared at the page for a very long time.

Cassie Roberts' headshot smiled out at him, and the editorial taunted him with her perfect life. Her dinner dates with her new boyfriend were well-documented in her reviews, as were her talented children who she also roped in as her cutesy Spy companions. There she was, telling the world about her upcoming birthday dinner at Le Bijou Bistro. *As if anyone cares,* Myles thought. And then it hit him. The perfect solution to get Cassie out of the way, and finish his novel in one fell swoop.

He didn't even need to come up with a plan, because the blueprint had been in his head for years. In his unfinished book, Murder at Table 12, he'd already plotted and planned the perfect mystery of how an unsuspecting guest was murdered at dinner. Fate had brought him to this point in his life, a chance to finish the book and finally write the ending that had eluded him for so long. He knew the staff at Le Bijou Bistro, so it wouldn't be difficult to set the wheels in motion.

Cassie Roberts was just going to be the real-life victim.

CHAPTER TWO

Al called room service as soon as he and Cassie arrived back at their suite at The Four Seasons Hotel. The town car he had at his disposal had taken them from the restaurant to the hotel in a matter of minutes.

"I need coffee up here now, lots of it," Al said in a low voice into the receiver, before replacing the handset with a click.

"Not for me, darling," Cassie said, looking over at him and shaking her head. "I just want to call it a night. That was quite a shock. I'm sorry for freaking out like that outside the restaurant, but this is one birthday I won't easily forget."

Al walked across the room to where Cassie was starting to remove her clothes and put on a hotel robe. It swamped her petite frame, and she wrapped the cord twice around her waist and tied it before rolling up the sleeves.

"Hey," he said, pulling her close. Cassie's head barely reached his chest. His wife of less than two weeks wrapped her slender arms around him, and he silently rocked her in an embrace until her trembling body stilled.

When she eventually raised her face to his, Al leaned down and planted several delicate kisses across her forehead and cheeks.

"C'mere, and sit down," he said, wiping away a tear from below her eye with his thumb, and guiding her toward the lounge area by the window, with its sweeping views over Elliott Bay and Puget Sound. Cassie shivered, and Al pressed a button, causing flames to start dancing in the fireplace mounted in the wall.

Al eased Cassie onto the sumptuous gold-colored sofa. There was a rap on the door, and Cassie looked up with a start. "S'okay, it's only the coffee," Al said, striding across the carpeted floor, and putting his hand in his pocket to get out a tip. He closed one eye and looked through the peephole before opening the door. Taking the tray from the waiter without letting him enter their room, Al tipped him, closed the door, and turned the lock. Returning moments later, he set the tray down with a thump on the low dark wood table.

"Jes' take a sip for ol' Al," he told her when he'd poured two cups of coffee and sat back down beside Cassie, handing her one of them. He waited until she'd taken a sip from the cup. "Atta girl," Al said with an encouraging smile. "We gotta talk, and this can't wait. So Ima gonna start, okay?"

Cassie nodded, her eyes wide.

Al took a deep breath before beginning. "Thing is, like I told ya' before, I done things in my past that ain't pretty. Can't go changin' any of that now. But there's a coupla' people I can think of who might be happy if Al De Duco was six feet under. Or his wife, for that matter. Ya' know what I mean?"

Cassie gasped.

"Now don't go jumpin' to conclusions," Al said. "Ain't nothin' or nobody gonna hurt ya' with me around. Thing is, we gotta be sensible and think this through. It's possible that woman fallin' down dead like that had nothin' to do with us. But then again…"

Cassie put her cup down and reached out for Al's hand. "Al, I know you're no saint, and I was aware of what I was letting myself in for when I agreed to marry you." She raised an eyebrow. "The reality might just be sinking in, but that doesn't change how I feel about you. I need to toughen up a bit, that's all. I'm not usually so emotional, but I think the champagne went to my head a little this evening."

Al grinned. "Yer' doin' great," he said, his beefy hand gently covering hers. "Best wife a guy coulda' wished fer. Don'tcha doubt that fer a second. Thing is, somethin's tellin' me that murder tonight, if it was in fact a murder, was too close to us to be a coincidence. Ima gonna' check out the people that might be gunnin' fer yours truly, but is there anyone ya' can think of, might have it in fer ya'?"

Cassie stared at Al in confusion. "What on earth do you mean? Why would someone want to kill me?"

Al rubbed his forehead. "I dunno. But ya' gotta think hard 'bout this. Do ya' have any enemies, or people with a grudge against ya', might wanna see ya' dead?"

Cassie's face crumpled. "Good grief. Not that I know of. Then again, I don't suppose Johnny thought so either, and look what happened to him." Johnny Roberts was Cassie's former husband, who had been murdered on a golf course in Whistler the previous year. Cassie pulled her hand away from Al and raised her arms, pressing her palms hard against her temples. "I can't believe this is happening. I wonder if Jake and DeeDee could help us. They have a lot of experience in this type of thing. If we could find out more about the woman who died, and if it really was murder, that would be a start."

"I was jes' thinkin' the same thing," Al said, in a soothing tone. "Ima gonna' give Jake a call and see what he can find out from his source in the police department. And that guy Rob that works with him is a genius when it comes to gettin' information 'bout people. Thing is, Rob's gotta have somethin' to go on. I need ya' to rack yer' brains 'bout anyone ya' might have upset lately, that could want ya' outta the way."

Cassie gripped Al's knee. "I know I've upset my daughter," she said, her voice shaking. She lowered her head. "Our marriage has disturbed her more than I ever could have imagined."

Al leaned over and smoothed Cassie's hair. "Briana ain't no murderer. That child loves ya' more than life itself. She's jes' hurtin' is all. She'll come around, I'm sure of it. It's jes' gonna take time. Ima thinkin' more along the lines of people ya' mighta' rubbed up the wrong way with one of yer' restaurant reviews. Ya' didn't mince yer' words on some of them bad'uns. How 'bout someone at the newspaper, that kinda' thing?"

Cassie shrugged sadly. "I don't know. I can write down the names of the restaurants I reviewed critically, if that helps. But I don't really know anyone at the paper, apart from Gloria Ekenbach, the Lifestyle Editor, and she seems really pleased with how things are going."

"Okay," Al said, taking some hotel stationery and a pen from a drawer. He handed them to Cassie. "Here ya' go. Jes' put it all down, whatever ya' can think of. I'll ask Rob to run checks on all of 'em." He paused, and scratched his head. "How about the guy yer' standin' in fer at The Seattle Times, Myles whats-his-face?"

Cassie looked up. "You mean Myles Lambert? I've never even met him."

"Don't matter none," Al said, rubbing his chin. "Put him on the list, and I'll see what Rob comes up with. Anyone else ya' can think of, and I don't care if it's someone whose fender ya' mighta bent outta shape, put 'em down as well, okay?"

Cassie nodded and picking up the pen, she began to write.

"Good girl," Al smiled. "Ima gonna call Jake and let him know what we're doin'. If he can talk to his police contact and have Rob on standby, we can get the names to him right away. Won't be long."

Al pulled his phone from his pocket and turned away from Cassie, striding towards the bedroom. His mind was working overtime. Jake wasn't the only person he needed to contact.

There were two people from Al's not-so-distant past that had trouble written all over them. First up was Mario Carlucci. His long-time grudge against Al had showed no sign of waning. The last Al had heard about him, Mario had been making inquiries about Al's whereabouts when he'd briefly relocated to the Caymans. Maybe Mario had learned Al was back in Seattle. Al knew a few people who could tell him whether or not that was the case.

The second person worried him even more. Scrolling through his phone, there were texts he'd received from Kitten Knight as recently as the week before. He'd told Cassie all about Kitten, an ex-girlfriend he'd never been serious about. Kitten seemed to think he'd led her to believe otherwise, and that he'd made promises to her he hadn't kept. Al was far more concerned about what Kitten was capable of than Mario.

*****

Cassie heard Al's gruff voice on the phone in the bedroom, as she scribbled the few names she could think of on the hotel stationery. Cassie had been brought up with hippy parents and lived by the motto of 'Love and Peace,' so she found it hard to fathom that anyone could hate another human being enough to kill them. Especially not over a restaurant review. For that reason, her list of names was short. She remembered several people she'd had run-ins with over the years, including a woman at her previous job at the Seattle Art Museum, and the mother of a friend of Briana's, who'd never liked her much. She added them both as an afterthought. When she was finished, she poured herself more coffee and sat back on the sofa, her eyes following the flames in the fireplace.

She knew Al was right, but she couldn't get the last words her daughter had said to her out of her head.

"I will never forgive you for doing this," Briana had seethed after Cassie and Al's short marriage ceremony at The Chapel of Love in Las Vegas.

The fact her children had agreed to come to Las Vegas for Al's surprise proposal had led Cassie to believe they were supportive of the marriage. While it turned out her son, Liam, was not delighted about it, his words were kinder than Briana's. "If it makes you happy, Mom," was all he'd said about the wedding.

Cassie knew it was quite soon after Johnny had died, and people might think she married Al on the rebound. But when Al had gotten down on one knee, she knew it was one hundred percent right. She'd never been more certain of anything in her life. She never doubted for a second that Al was her second chance for happiness. Nor did she question how lucky she was to have been blessed by true love again after a twenty-something-year marriage. All of her instincts told her to seize the moment with Al, because she knew first-hand how lives and circumstances could change in a heartbeat.

Her daughter Briana had adored her father, and was still heartbroken by his death. Cassie wanted nothing more than to help her daughter through her grief, and for her to understand that Cassie marrying Al did not diminish her former love for Johnny, or tarnish his memory in any way. But Briana had rejected Cassie's pleas to listen to her, and left Las Vegas right after the ceremony. Briana hadn't returned any of her mother's calls in the past ten days.

Cassie's thoughts were interrupted by the sound of Al yelling from the direction of the bathroom. He sounded panicked. "CASSIE!!"

She jumped up and ran through the bedroom, stopping to remove the pistol from the drawer of her bedside table, where Al had placed it when he moved in after their marriage. He'd explained that it was necessary because of his past, and he'd trained her how to use the gun during several trips to a firing range.

"Yer' not a bad shot," he'd said as he complimented her with pride after the second lesson at the pistol range. "I'd be scared if ya' were pointing that thing at me."

Cassie ran into the bathroom, her hands holding the gun steady, pointing it like she'd learned, having no idea of what she'd find. Her husband was cowering in the corner, his back against the wall.

"Over there." Al's voice was low, and he nodded at the black creature in the bathtub. "I thought ya' was gonna speak to Housekeeping. That's the second time in a week one of 'em has been in the tub."

Cassie put the gun down with a sigh. She leaned into the bathtub and scooped the spider up in her hands. "This little thing? It's tiny, Al." She held her cupped hands out for Al to look, but he was backing out of the room.

"Kill it," he ordered, his deep voice returning.

"It's unlucky to kill a spider," Cassie said softly.

"Yep. Unlucky fer' the spider," Al said, leaving the room as quickly as he could.

Cassie smiled, and opened the window quietly. Letting the spider go, she closed the window again before flushing the toilet.

"All gone," she called to her husband. "Down the drain. It's safe to come back in here."

CHAPTER THREE

Kitten Knight pulled her jacket across her shoulders and smiled at the waiter who was approaching with her cocktail balanced on a tray he was holding in his hand. Sitting on the open air patio of The Nest Bar at The Thompson Hotel, a dozen stories above Puget Sound, the postcard panoramic view came at the price of a cutting March afternoon breeze. She reached her hand up to tuck several stray platinum hairs into the braid that was twisted around in a loose knot at the back of her head. It was a style she'd seen models wearing on the runways in New York that season, and when she'd returned to Seattle, she'd shown her hair stylist the photograph she'd taken of it. Kitten wanted her to replicate it. Kitten changed her hair styles like some people change their shoes, and she had an entire closet devoted to elaborate hairpieces and accessories.

"Thank you," she said to the waiter as he set the chunky highball glass on the table, her voice a soft purr. A well-practiced flutter of her eyelashes, a hint of a pout, and two twenty-dollar bills pressed into his hand, she'd learned a long time ago, would ensure a waiter's attention for the rest of her visit. She stirred her Mojito with the black straw that came with the drink, causing the ice to clink in the glass before raising it to her scarlet lips and taking a long sip through the straw. The chilled white rum, laced with lime juice and an infusion of mint leaves was a refreshing way to start the day. Although it was after three in the afternoon, Kitten always slept past noon, and never ate before dinner, her one meal of the day. It was a routine she'd followed since her performing days, twenty-five years earlier, and the way things worked out, she didn't see any reason to change.

Kitten's sister, Maureen, came tottering across the patio, laden with shopping bags from several of the nearby department stores. Setting her bags down, she waved for the waiter before leaning down to graze Kitten's cheek with her lips. Then Maureen reached for Kitten's drink and emptied half of its contents in two big gulps.

"Hey..." Kitten protested, but Maureen held the glass out of reach. The waiter appeared within seconds, and Kitten ordered a jug of Mojitos and a fresh glass.

Maureen beamed. "Can you believe that dude in the gray suit outside the elevator just carded me? I know I look good, but please, I don't think I look that young."

Kitten's face was expressionless, the result of her regular botox maintenance several days earlier. "The guy with the earpiece? Maybe he has a thing for older women. You do look great, Maureen, but you're over fifty."

"Hmm." Maureen settled in her chair, eyeing her younger sister. "You're only a couple of years behind me. Although ever since you went to the same plastic surgeon as Kim Kardashian, I'm not sure I recognize you anymore. Is my Kitty still in there, somewhere?"

Kitten smiled. "Of course. Maybe it's because I never married or had children, that the years have been kind to me. I might have had a few tweaks to my face, but my body is all natural."

Maureen frowned. "Apart from the breasts, you mean, and the liposuction?"

They paused while the waiter returned to the table with their drink order.

"Lipo isn't like having work done. I consider it to be body

maintenance," Kitten retorted. She reached for her drink. "And my boob job is ancient history." She peered down at her ample cleavage. "Anyway, I had to do the augmentation for work and it was tax-deductible, might I add."

Despite the cosmetic help she may have had, Kitten's years as a burlesque dancer had been good to her body. Even though she hadn't performed on stage in a long time, she still went to regular dance classes, ballet being her passion. As a teenager, she'd grown too tall to be a professional ballet dancer, and in any case, her father, an actuary for a pension fund company, had vetoed what he called 'any silly dancing nonsense.' He'd wanted both of his daughters to attend college. Maureen had complied, but Kitten had rebelled.

Maureen rolled her eyes. "You know you broke daddy's heart. The day he saw your name in lights on the marquee of that crummy little strip club where you first started working was the day the light in his own eyes went out. He was never the same again. I think the shame got him before the cancer did."

Kitten leaned across to her sister with an icy stare. "You might have been a goodie-two-shoes and done everything daddy said, and where did it get you? Two ex-husbands just like him, and you weren't able to speak your mind till you hit fifty and finally came to your senses. Glad to see you're making up for it now, though. At least I made my own way and knew my own mind."

"If sleeping with rich men is making your own way, then I guess you're right," Maureen said with a giggle, setting her heavy based glass down on the table and reaching for the Mojito jug. Kitten held hers out for a refill, and Maureen began to pour. "Speaking of which, I saw a friend of yours the other day." She gave Kitten a sly wink.

Kitten's eye narrowed. "Who would that be?"

Maureen discarded her straw, and lifted the glass to her mouth. "Oh, you know. The big old sexy guy you're so taken with. I think his name's Al something-or-other. You know, the one with the scar and the goofy smile."

Kitten sat back in her chair, watching Maureen, and said nothing for several moments. The sisters had an uneasy relationship. Although they saw each other regularly since they were each other's only family apart from Maureen's adult children, there was still a sibling rivalry between them that had existed ever since childhood. After Kitten had left home and been shunned by her parents for her chosen career, she'd envied Maureen's closeness to them, especially their father. For many years, she'd suspected Maureen had felt stifled by conformity and regretted having lived her life for other people. Now a well-off divorcee, Maureen had only started to come out of her shell in middle age. But if Maureen really had seen Al De Duco, Kitten wanted to know all about it.

"Are you sure? A few months ago he moved to the Cayman Islands. In fact, I was planning on visiting him there, so I'm surprised you saw him here in Seattle."

"Oh, I'm sure, all right," Maureen said. She sucked in her cheeks. "But I don't think you'll be visiting him, when you hear what he's been up to."

Kitten didn't like the smug smile that was plastered all over her sister's face. She tried to stay calm, wondering what Maureen could be referring to. Kitten and Al had been an off and on item for quite a few years. They had an understanding, and a good time dating whenever it suited Al. Kitten had several other wealthy suitors, and between them all, she enjoyed a nice lifestyle. She lived in a very upscale condominium, paid for from several Las Vegas homes she'd owned back in her heyday.

Her suitors paid for meals out and holidays, along with generous gifts of designer clothes, shoes, and sometimes jewelry. The small sum Kitten had inherited when her father died remained untouched, the lion's share of his estate having gone to her mother and Maureen. Now that their mother had dementia and required around-the-clock care, it was likely there would be nothing else coming her way when her mother died.

"What do you mean, what he's been up to?" Kitten said, laughing lightly. "He must be back in town on business. I should call him and find out for myself." She was free later that evening, so she decided she'd do just that. She'd felt bad for Al ever since his boss Vinny had been murdered in what initially looked like a gangland hit. She knew he blamed himself for not being able to prevent Vinny's death.

"Oh, you know," Maureen said, staring straight at Kitten. She paused, before dropping her bombshell. "He got married."

Kitten's jaw dropped, and she had to steady her hand or her glass would have dropped too. She wanted to slap that stupid smirk off of Maureen's face, but desperate for more information, she forced herself to retain her composure. During the time she'd been with Al, he'd never been available to settle down, because his work took him wherever Vinny went. A time or two they'd talked about the future, and Kitten had enjoyed hearing about Al's dreams of retiring to the Cayman Islands. She'd thought it sounded idyllic, if a little dull, and often joked about joining him there. Al had said she'd be welcome any time. She'd always taken that as an open invitation to visit him whenever she wanted to. And if she'd decided to stay on…well, she'd always assumed that was a possibility too.

Maureen reached into one of her shopping bags and pulled out a copy of that day's newspaper. "Here," she said, handing it to Kitten, who looked confused. Maureen was pointing at the restaurant review page. "Look, it's all there."

"What on earth has this got to do with Al?" Kitten asked, glancing down at the paper.

"That's who he got married to," Maureen said, patiently. "The woman who's the new Food Spy. I saw him at the auction house when I was having a painting appraised. He was telling me all about her, what she did, and stuff like that. He was very pleased with himself. Said they were just back from their wedding in Vegas. Oh, by the way, he asked about you and sends his regards."

Kitten's hands were shaking as she scanned the newspaper article Maureen had given her. The restaurant reviewer, a woman by the name of Cassie Roberts, gave a lot of personal details in the food column she wrote which read more like a journal. The writer's thoughts about food were overshadowed by anecdotes about her darling new husband, and their plans for her upcoming birthday celebration at Le Bijou Bistro.

An angry mist descended over Kitten, hurt beyond belief by how Al had treated her. Her chest tightened, and she was shocked at the realization that she would have loved to be Mrs. De Duco, if she'd ever known it was an option. Instead, this Cassie Roberts woman had stepped in and seduced Al at a time when he was vulnerable because of Vinny's death. And to top it all off, Cassie Smugface was parading her prize husband all over the press. Kitten threw the paper onto the table in disgust, looking past Maureen to the backdrop of islands, the Olympics, and ferries plowing through the Sound.

Maureen's voice interrupted the swirl of thoughts racing through Kitten's mind. "Kitten, are you—"

Kitten glanced at Maureen's worried face. "It's a bit late for concern, sister dearest. If you'll excuse me, I have a call to make." Kitten picked up her phone and walked across to the edge of the patio, where a chest-high clear barrier was the only thing that separated her from the rush hour traffic on First Avenue located far below from where she was standing.

The only way she'd be able to find out if she still had any place in his life was to speak to Al himself. Leaning against the barrier, she pressed his number. It went straight to voicemail.

"Hey, Al," she said sweetly. "Maureen told me you're in town. I believe congratulations are in order. Maybe we could hook up when you're free. I've been missing you, and you know what that means, baby. Mwah." She blew a kiss into the handset and ended the call.

Walking back to the table, she smiled to herself. There was no reason to let a small problem like a wife stand in the way of Kitten and her one true love. Now that she knew Al was the marrying type, she had to make him see that he'd married the wrong woman. By the time she got back to where Maureen was sitting, her phone pinged with a message from Al. She smiled to herself and knew everything was going to work out. Easing back into her chair, she crossed her legs. She knew Maureen's eyes were on her as she read the message from Al.

"Kitten, I'm not interested. I love my wife. Please don't contact me again. Take care of yourself, Al."

It took a few seconds for the message to sink in. Then, in a rush of adrenalin, Kitten knew what she had to do. No one dismissed Kitten Knight like that. Especially not when they'd treated her as badly as Al De Duco had just done. One little text, and Kitten would make sure Al would regret what he'd done to her for the rest of his life. If he loved this Cassie woman so much, Kitten wondered how he'd feel if his new little wifey wasn't around anymore. Kitten knew some people who could easily arrange for that to happen. She turned to Maureen with a conspiratorial smile.

"Silly old Al. I never liked him that much anyway. Do you see those two men over there? They've been looking at us ever since they arrived. What say we let them buy us some champagne?"

She raised her hand and waved to the men, who started walking towards them. Kitten was back in control, which was just how she liked things to be.

CHAPTER FOUR

"Looks like I timed that perfectly," Jake said as he sauntered into DeeDee's kitchen, her husky dog Balto at his heels, and kissed her on the cheek. "Is that bacon I smell cooking?"

Balto woofed.

"Balto's hungry after our walk on the beach," Jake said, pulling out a stool and sitting at the counter. "Me too, come to think of it. There's something about the fresh morning air and making calls about a murder. See? Balto's nodding. I can tell he agrees with me."

DeeDee turned away from the stove and placed one of her hands on her hip. "I've never known you two not to be hungry. How about Red? Have you taken care of him?"

Red, Al's Doberman Pinscher, was staying with DeeDee while Al and Cassie were temporarily living at The Four Seasons Hotel. It made sense, since DeeDee had plenty of outdoor space and lived near the beach. Balto and Red weren't really playmates, but they had a healthy respect for one another. DeeDee suspected Red wasn't impressed by Balto's adoration for Al, Red's master, and there was a bit of a doggy rivalry going on.

Jake nodded. "Yep, he's fed and watered." He poured a glass of orange juice from the jug on the countertop. "I spoke to Al while I was out," he said. Looking down at Balto, he laughed. "I swear that dog knows what we're saying. It used to just be the words 'ferry' and 'food' that set him off. Now, you only have to mention 'Al', and he's spinning around like he's chasing his tail. See what I mean?"

DeeDee looked down at Balto, who was circling Jake's stool with gusto.

"Lie down, Balto," she commanded. Balto hesitated. He looked over at her with his one brown eye and one blue eye, before falling to the floor.

"Good boy," DeeDee said, walking over and rewarding him with a small piece of bacon.

"Hey, what about me?" Jake protested. "I'm a good boy, too."

DeeDee grinned, and leaned in to kiss him. "I know you are. Yours is coming." Her lips lingered on his, and she had to tear herself back to the stove before the bacon burned. Jake groaned. "I can wait for breakfast if that's an alternative."

DeeDee smiled to herself as she dished out two plates of bacon, avocado, and poached eggs on sourdough toast. Things had been going great with Jake since their break-up at the start of the year, when they'd spent some time apart. "Nice try, buster, but I thought you had a possible murder to solve."

She joined Jake at the counter, where she served their breakfast. Pouring coffee for both of them, she asked, "What did Al have to say?"

"He wanted to know if I'd talked to my contact at the Seattle Police Department," Jake said, between bites of his eggs and bacon.

"And have you?"

Jake's eyes widened. "It's only 10:00 in the morning. A woman died at the table our friends were supposed to be dining at last night.

There were whispers as we were leaving the restaurant that she was murdered. What do you think?"

DeeDee tilted her head to one side. "Hmm, I'd say you probably made that call several hours ago."

"You'd be right. After everything Al has done for us, the least I can do is help him sort this thing out. I'm glad he asked us. Although, I'd be grateful if you didn't go chasing after suspects like you usually do. Leave that to Al and me."

DeeDee knew Jake was referring to several close escapes she'd had in previous murder investigations in which they'd been involved. For some unknown reason, murder seemed to follow her around. She was almost getting used to it, although that wasn't to say she liked it.

"I promise," she said solemnly. "Anyway, what did you find out from the police?"

Jake's sparkling blue eyes rested on hers. "Seems like the whispers could be right. Initial indications from the coroner are that the woman was poisoned, but that still has to be confirmed."

DeeDee raised her hand to her mouth. "Oh, how horrible. Who was she?"

Jake rubbed his chin. "Her name was Megan Reilly. She was twenty-eight years old and dining with her boyfriend, Luke Robertson. It turns out he's a Seattle cop. His coworkers at the Police Department are pretty upset about it, as you can imagine. Given the circumstances, there's going to be a lot of heat on this case. As soon as they learn anything else, my contact will let me know. In the meantime, he gave me Luke's number so I can get in touch with him directly."

DeeDee sipped her coffee in silence. The reality of their lucky escape the previous evening was beginning to sink in. To think that it might have been her friend Cassie who had died...she shuddered.

"Al said he spoke to Rob first thing this morning," Jake continued, "and asked him to check out some names Cassie thought of last night."

"You mean, people that might want to kill her?"

Jake nodded. "The thing is, Al told me he thinks Cassie's in denial. She's finding it hard to believe anyone would want to kill her for something she's done. He's inclined to agree with her. He thinks if Cassie was the intended victim, it's more likely someone was trying to kill him as well, or get at Cassie as revenge on him for his past."

DeeDee pushed her plate away.

"Don't you want to finish that?" Jake said, staring at her half-eaten breakfast.

DeeDee shook her head, and pushed it over to him. "Did Al have any ideas who might be after him?"

Jake gave a piece of bacon to Balto, who was hovering at his feet. "Yes, he said there were a couple of people, but he didn't share any details. Just said that he would deal with it. My concern is...no, never mind."

Jake's crinkled brow indicated to DeeDee he wasn't happy about something. She pressed him for more information. "What do you mean, Jake?"

Jake thought for a few moments, leaning his elbow on the counter and resting his chin on his fist. "Let's see...how shall I put this? I suspect Al's way of dealing with things might be a little more reckless than you or I would care for. Al's kind of a law unto himself. He thinks nothing of taking justice into his own hands. If we find out who killed Megan, and that someone had meant to murder Cassie or Al, he won't be waiting for the police to put the killer behind bars."

DeeDee's voice was a whisper. "You think Al would kill them? But then he could go to jail, and that would break Cassie's heart.

She's been through enough, what with Johnny dying, and now this."

Jake shrugged. "Hopefully, it won't come to that. I'll try my best to keep an eye on him, but he's a loose cannon. I have no idea who the people are he was referring to, so I'm pretty much in the dark." He took the last bite of his toast, and stood up. "I'll clear these things up while you finish your coffee."

DeeDee watched Jake take the dishes over to the sink. She noticed Balto had stirred from where he'd been sitting at the foot of Jake's stool, and was on alert in the kitchen doorway. She exchanged a look with Jake, as the sound of a car pulling up outside reached them. Balto went mad with excitement when he heard footsteps approaching the front door, and he bolted out through the hallway in that direction.

DeeDee grinned at Jake. "There's only one man Balto goes quite that crazy for. I mean, he likes you, Jake, but you know you've been relegated from his No. 1 Guy spot, right?"

With a smirk, Jake put down the dishcloth he was holding and said, "I'll let Al in."

CHAPTER FIVE

"Are you sure you're feeling all right, sweetheart? You've hardly eaten a thing."

Mario Carlucci looked across the table to where his dinner date, Kitten Knight, was idly pushing around the food on her plate with her fork. The lighting in Canlis restaurant was dim, and the glow from the candle in the glass jar on the table was kind to Kitten, whose appearance was less put-together than usual. Her long, thick platinum braid had come loose from where it had been wrapped at the back of her head earlier in the evening, and snaked down one shoulder. Kitten's eyes were smudged with eyeliner and mascara that looked as if it had been rubbed out of place, and her trademark scarlet lips were misshapen, perhaps due to trying to apply her lipstick with an unsteady hand, the same one that now gripped her wine glass as if her life depended on it.

Kitten took a swig of wine and stared at Mario, her glassy eyes lifeless. She shrugged. "I'm here, aren't I? I thought that's what you wanted."

A slow, easy smile crossed Mario's face. High-maintenance women like Kitten needed careful handling, but he'd had years of practice. It was a fine line between treating them mean and then showering them with affection and baubles. It was time to reel her in. Judging by the mood she was in tonight, maybe she'd had enough of his games. The other women he'd been seeing weren't even in the same league as Kitten, and he didn't want to lose her.

Mario's hand reached for Kitten's knee under the table. "You know I love spending time with you. I was delighted when you called earlier to say you were at The Nest and in need of some company. Goodness knows, you saved me from a boring meeting with my bankers." His hand edged up Kitten's warm leg, under the hem of her skirt, and he felt her squirm back in her seat.

Undeterred, Mario kept talking. "The thing is, there's been something I've been meaning to ask you. I was thinking it's about time we became exclusive. What do you say?" He beamed at her expectantly.

Kitten's eyes flickered, but her face gave nothing away. Mario had been hoping for a more positive reaction. There were plenty of women who would jump at an offer like that, but Kitten wasn't like other women. That's what he loved about her.

Mario leaned in closer to her. If Kitten wanted to play hard to get, he had it covered. "There's a penthouse with your name on it at Waterfront Palace, my new property development. The interior designer is on standby for you to consult with. However you want to do the furnishings and decor is entirely up to you. It's a blank canvas, and the budget's very generous, within reason of course."

Kitten's gaze remained blank. "Can I think it over?" She pushed his hand away from her leg, and stood up, picking up her purse. "Excuse me, I'll just be a moment."

Mario inhaled. Kitten had some nerve. Maybe it would take more than an apartment for her to commit to him. He watched her sashay towards the ladies room, albeit slightly unsteady on her feet. She'd called him after 7:00 p.m., and judging by how her speech was slurring, he guessed she must have been in The Nest for several hours before that. When he'd picked her up outside The Thompson Hotel in his Porsche, she'd been laughing and giggling with her sister Maureen. Mario had hailed a cab for Maureen, a flirty middle-aged woman who wasn't a beauty like her sister, but had a bubbly personality after a few drinks. When Mario had met her on previous occasions, he thought Maureen had a mean streak that was often directed towards Kitten. If he were a betting man, he would have said Maureen was jealous of her younger sister.

The waiter arrived at the table to clear the dishes. He lifted Kitten's plate, which had barely been touched. "Was everything satisfactory with your meal, Mr. Carlucci?"

Mario looked up. "Yes, thank you. My companion wasn't very hungry. My filet mignon was delicious, as always. Please, give my compliments to the chef."

Mario's eyes wandered around the room as he waited for Kitten to return. Canlis was a dressy, upscale dining restaurant, and its clientele looked the part. Ladies wore the latest styles and expensive jewelry, and the men wore suits or sport coats. He glanced over at several people he knew, nodding to them in recognition. The place was buzzing, and deservedly so. Canlis was frequently recognized as one of best restaurants in the United States.

Mario dined there often and was a generous tipper, so the staff had been known to find him a table on short notice, such as this particular evening. The fact that someone else's reservation may have been bumped, and they had to wait at the bar, didn't concern Mario. Growing up in a crime family had given him an expectation of always getting what he wanted. It had been a long time since he'd killed anyone, not since his father died and the family had gone legit. But he still had a gun, and he wasn't afraid to use it.

When Kitten reappeared, her hair had been secured behind her head once more, and her eye makeup and lipstick were no longer smudged. She took a sip of water, reaching across the table for Mario's hand.

Clutching her palm to his, Mario could feel her clammy skin.

"Mario, please don't take this the wrong way, but I won't be able to take you up on your offer. It's very generous, but it's…I just can't." There were tears forming in her eyes, and Mario reached into his pocket, handing her a freshly laundered monogrammed linen handkerchief.

"Kitten, there's no need to decide now," he said, worried. He could tell this wasn't a bluff by Kitten. "I can tell you're not yourself tonight. Take as long as you need. The interior designer, Briana Roberts, will be on site for the next few days and can show you around any time." He squeezed her hand. "Oh, and I was thinking that old VW of yours has seen better days. I'll have one of my team bring a lease car over for you in the morning."

Kitten started to protest. "Mario, I—"

"Nonsense. Not much, just a Mercedes or something. No strings. Keep it as long as you like."

Kitten shook her head so hard that the braid on her head came undone once more. "Mario, you're not listening to me. You're a fine man, and a kind person, but I won't deceive you. I don't love you. You deserve to find someone who does."

Mario's face hardened. Kitten tried to pull her hand away from his, but he held onto her with a tight grip. There was only one explanation why Kitten would turn him down. And he wanted to hear it direct from her.

"He's back, isn't he?" Mario's voice was low and menacing. "That idiot, Al De Duco."

Kitten said nothing, but the look on her face told Mario all he needed to know. Kitten wasn't the first woman he'd lost because of Al De Duco. He felt a twinge in his chest. Even though it had been thirty years ago, the pain of having his first love, Lola Forte, cruelly taken from him had never waned.

Mario and Lola had been childhood sweethearts in Chicago, both from crime families who worked for the "the Outfit." Lola was a newly-certified kindergarten teacher, and Mario had just finished his engineering degree, when he proposed to her on their first trip abroad to Venice, Italy. When Mario got down on bended knee, the gondola they were traveling in had wobbled so much it almost capsized. He could never remember a day since then when he'd laughed so much or felt as happy. Lola and Mario planned to go back to Venice on their honeymoon the following year, after a large family wedding in Chicago.

"You're thinking about Lola, aren't you?" Kitten said sadly. "I know how much you loved her. That's what it should be like, Mario. Don't settle for anything less. You and I have fun together, but let's not pretend it's anything more than that."

Mario dropped Kitten's hand, gazing out the windows of Canlis at the city and the water of the Sound beyond. Mario had everything money could buy, but inside he still felt hollow. He was able to fill his days with work, and at night there was no shortage of beautiful women to occupy the space on the other side of his bed. Kitten was the only woman since Lola he'd considered getting serious with. And once again, Mario had Al De Duco to thank for ruining his chance at happiness. He thought he'd gotten away from Al when he left Chicago, only to find Al and Vinny had also moved to Seattle in recent years.

Kitten's voice cut through his thoughts. "It wasn't Al's fault, what happened to Lola. He told me about it."

Mario motioned to the waiter to bring the check. His tone was cold and businesslike. "I've had enough of this conversation. Why you're sticking up for that man, I have no idea. So tell me, have you seen him? Last I heard, he'd retired to the Caymans. Best place for him, as far as I'm concerned."

Kitten sucked in her cheeks and stared coolly at Mario before she looked away. "No," she said softly. "I haven't seen him. Maureen bumped into him at an auction house. He told her he'd gotten married."

Mario watched Kitten dab her eyes again with his handkerchief. She went to hand it back to him, but he waved her away. "Keep it," he said, more gently. He handed his black Amex card to the waiter, and waited to resume the conversation until after the waiter had left.

"Kitten, my offer still stands. I won't let you down like Al did. Maybe what you and I have together isn't love, but like you said, two lonely people with a lot of respect for each other can still have a lot of fun together. And who's to say it won't grow into something more? I'm willing to give it a shot if you are. All I ask is that you don't rule it out for now. What do you say?"

Kitten bowed her head. Mario tried one last time. "Look, I'll tell you what. How about I give you some space for a while, then we go away next week to that place in the country you love, and talk it over again. We can leave Wednesday. It's quiet there midweek. That's a plan, right?"

Kitten glared at Mario. "I can't do it on Wednesday. I have something to deal with that night." She waved to the waiter and asked him to call her a cab.

"I'll take you home, baby," Mario protested, but Kitten stood up.

She leaned down and kissed Mario briefly on the lips, pausing to whisper in his ear. "If you have any sense at all Mario, you won't wait for my call. I'm not sure what's going to happen after next week, but I might be going away for a long time. Goodbye."

Mario sat alone at the table for a long time, not in any hurry to make his way home alone. Nursing a whisky, it was thoughts of Lola, not Kitten, that drifted through his mind. The night she died would be etched in his memory forever. At least he'd made it to the scene in time to hold her hand and comfort her while she bled to death, shot several times in the abdomen.

He'd been on his way to pick her up from her family home when he got a call saying that Lola, her brother Charlie, and Vinny Santora had just been hit at a take-out pizza joint in Chicago. They'd gotten their pizzas and were standing on the sidewalk in front of the pizza joint waiting for Al De Duco to pick them up, when a car pulled up next to them and shots rang out.

Al De Duco, who was supposed to be driving them home, had arrived at the pizza place minutes after the shooting, only to find all three of them wounded. The two men survived, but unfortunately Lola died at the scene with Mario kneeling on the sidewalk next to her. As it turned out, Al had been delayed because he'd stopped on the way to pick up cigars as a surprise for Vinny. Otherwise, they all would have been out of there before the gunmen arrived.

Finishing his whiskey with a gulp, Mario decided it was time to get those memories out of his head once and for all. The only way to ever get over Lola's death was to settle the score with Al De Duco. Mario could find out where he was living easily enough. A slow, painful death, like Lola had suffered, was no less than the man deserved. Then, with Al gone, there would be no one standing in the way between Mario and Kitten.

A smile returned to Mario's face. He was a man with a plan, and that's just how he liked to do business.

CHAPTER SIX

A stony-faced Al entered the kitchen with his arm around a pale and drawn looking Cassie. As usual, Balto was glued to Al's heels.

DeeDee took one look at her friend and rose from her seat at the counter. "Let's go into the great room, Cassie, where it's more comfortable, and leave these two men alone to do whatever it is they need to do."

Cassie looked up at Al, who nodded, and gave her a reassuring smile. "Ima gonna' talk with Jake about a plan of action. Ya' go on with DeeDee fer now. Right, Jake?"

Jake looked up from the coffeemaker where he was just finishing brewing a fresh pot of coffee and said, "I think that's a good idea. You two go and sit down. I'll be through in a moment."

"And we need cake," DeeDee reminded him. "Lots of cake."

Al adjusted his sunglasses. "Yer' in the right place fer cake, Cassie. I can vouch for that."

"That's settled then," DeeDee said, ushering Cassie out of the kitchen and into the hallway, where she paused to give her a big hug. "This is all going to be okay," she said, "although I realize it doesn't seem that way now. If anyone is out to harm you or Al, he and Jake will make sure nothing happens to either one of you."

Cassie followed DeeDee into the great room. It was a bright spring morning, and DeeDee had the windows open, allowing a light flow of fresh air to circulate into the room. The view outside, past the garden, and over the trail to the beach, was dotted with early spring wildflowers starting to bloom, beyond which Puget Sound was a calm, inviting deep blue.

"Thanks, DeeDee. Al also said something along those lines," Cassie said with a tight smile, settling onto the sofa. "Except, he didn't put it quite so politely."

DeeDee sat opposite Cassie in an armchair. Cassie involuntarily shivered, and DeeDee stood up. "Sorry, Cassie. I'll close the windows."

Cassie waved her down. "No, please, I'm not cold. I love the feel of the fresh air flowing through here. I felt claustrophobic at the hotel, so I really am enjoying it. Al was so concerned about me, he wouldn't leave me alone for a minute."

"Yo. Walls have ears, ya' know."

DeeDee and Cassie both turned to where Al was standing in the doorway. He smiled, standing back to let Jake walk past him with a tray filled with a coffee pot, mugs, and several slices of cake.

"I skipped the chocolate cake," Jake said, setting the tray down in front of Cassie and DeeDee. "I understand that's what the poor woman who died choked on last night."

Cassie gave him a pointed look. "In that case, I think I'll be skipping chocolate cake for a very long time. I'm really sorry, because it's my favorite."

Cassie's words hung in the air, as the gravity of her statement sunk in for all of them. The flapping wings of a flock of birds as they flew past the window was the only sound that could be heard. DeeDee exchanged a look with Jake, and noticed Cassie and Al doing the same.

Jake was the first to speak. "Let's get started on what we plan to do, because there's no time to waste. Al and I are going to go to Le Bijou Bistro this morning. We decided to talk to the staff before the lunchtime crowd starts arriving. They should be open by now for deliveries and setting up. My police contact told me that the forensic team finished their work up at the restaurant last night."

Al walked over to Cassie, and pulled out a heavy revolver, setting it on the arm of the sofa beside where she was sitting. "Cassie, I want you to stay here with DeeDee, and don't let this out of your sight. Got it?" His voice was encouraging, and he crouched down, his face hovering close to his wife's, before tenderly touching the back of her head and leaning in to kiss her.

Cassie smiled at Al's touch, and she nodded.

Al stood up and turned to DeeDee. "DeeDee, ya' better not upset Cassie. She's gotten to be a pretty good shot with that thing. Took the head clean off a target at the range the other day."

DeeDee tried not to giggle. The thought of Cassie shooting the head off of anything was hard to imagine, but she knew Cassie was level-headed and would do whatever was required for self-protection.

"In that case I'd better get my gun, too," DeeDee said.

Jake raised an eyebrow, taking DeeDee's gun from his inside coat pocket and handing it to her. "I beat you to it. It's fully loaded." His gaze passed from DeeDee to Cassie, then back again. "I hope I don't need to tell you both to be careful?"

"We will," DeeDee assured him.

"Good," Al said. "We'll be a coupla' hours at least. Balto's gonna stay in the house with ya', and Red's on guard outside. I'm tellin' ya' nobody, but nobody, gets past Red."

Balto growled as if he understood what Al had just said.

"Or Balto," Al said, leaning down to rub his thick black and white fur.

"We'll see you later," Jake said, as he leaned down and kissed DeeDee on the cheek. "I love you," he whispered in her ear, sending a tingle down her spine.

"Love you too," she mouthed as they began to leave. She stood up and followed Jake to the door. When they were out of the house she locked the door and engaged the deadbolt.

"Sit tight, Cassie," she said, "I won't be long." It took several minutes for her to go around the house, closing all the windows, and making sure they were secure. Her tour ended with her locking the door from the kitchen to the yard and picking up her cell phone from the kitchen counter where she'd left it. She carried it into the great room and set it down on the side table next to her gun. She looked over at Cassie, who was stroking Balto and said, "Well. This is certainly a strange situation for us to be in. A bit different from when we lived next door to each other on Mercer Island. Would you like some coffee?"

Cassie nodded. "Sure. But I'll pass on the cake, if you don't mind. Yours are the best, but I can't quite handle any right now."

DeeDee poured two mugs of coffee and after adding sugar and some cream to both of them, handed one to Cassie. She stared at the cake, then thought better of it. "I know what you mean. Even though I made it myself, I think I'll pass, too."

Cassie sipped her coffee, and DeeDee watched her visibly relax as she sat back in her chair. "Al and I are really grateful for you and Jake helping us like this," Cassie said. "Thank you."

"That's what friends are for, and I don't want to hear another word about it. How about Liam and Briana, do they know what's happened?"

Cassie's chin quivered, and she cupped both hands around her mug. "No," she said at last. "Liam's off taking photos in the jungles of Mexico. National Geographic has hired him for his first paid shoot, and he's out of contact right now. As for Briana...well, I don't want to worry her. There's no point until we know a little more."

DeeDee had the same feeling she'd had the night before, that Cassie was holding back something. "I understand," she said, wondering how to phrase her concerns. "I bet Briana's excited about your new home. I'm sure you'll want to put your own touch on it. Is your award-winning interior designer daughter going to help you with the decorating?"

"I doubt it. I haven't spoken to her since the wedding. It seems she's blocked my telephone number." Cassie sat forward, her posture becoming tense once more.

"Oh, Cassie. I'm sorry. Did she object to you marrying Al?"

Cassie shrugged. "She was there, but she didn't say anything until afterwards. I guess I didn't realize how hurt she was when I started seeing Al so soon after her father died. I've been so caught up in my own little bubble, I couldn't see how my marrying Al might affect my children. Maybe I was too hasty. I know I've disappointed her."

DeeDee's eyes widened. "Oh, no. Please don't tell me you've made a mistake. Al would be brokenhearted if he heard that. He adores you."

"Of course not." Cassie's eyes were shining. "After I met Al, I never doubted I'd be with him for the rest of my life. When we went to Las Vegas I had no idea what he was planning, and I certainly had no thought that I'd return to Seattle as a married woman. What I meant was, I got so carried away in the moment, it never occurred to me I should have talked to Liam and Briana about it. I think if I'd explained it to them, they would have understood a little better, and if I'd known how they felt, and especially Briana, maybe I would have persuaded Al that we should wait a while."

"Cassie, you're a grown woman," DeeDee reminded her. "I think you're being too hard on yourself. You don't need to ask your children's permission for anything."

"I know, and you're right. I think Liam is being pragmatic about it, certainly less emotional. But Briana made it very clear she thinks I've betrayed her in some way. I really thought she'd love Al once she got to know him, but she's never given him a chance. I just hope she accepts Al at some point, and I don't lose her over this. Al is my husband now, and that's not going to change, no matter what my daughter thinks."

DeeDee sighed. "I don't need to tell you that Briana was a daddy's girl. It's understandable that her nose is a little bent out of joint, but I'm sure she'll get over this and come to her senses. In the meantime, we need to get to the bottom of the death of Megan Reilly. So tell me, who were the suspects you came up with for Rob to check out? Jake told me you were struggling to think of anyone who would want to kill you."

There was the sound of a car driving past, and DeeDee and Cassie both froze. DeeDee held her breath as she reached for her gun. She got up and crept across the room to the edge of the window, where she stood with her back to the wall before turning her head to the side and daring to look out the window.

"It's just a car driving by," she said to Cassie, after looking in both directions. "It had nothing to do with us." She returned to her chair. "Now, where were we?"

"Suspects," Cassie said sighing. "What Jake told you was absolutely right. It was hard. Eventually we came up with three names, as well as a few restaurants I wrote bad reviews on. There were four of them."

"Let's get back to the three people you mentioned," DeeDee said. "I guess we need to see what Rob finds out, but there might be something you and I can do to help out with the investigation. Who were they?"

"The first one is Myles Lambert," Cassie said. "He's the guy whose column I'm covering at The Seattle Times while he's on a temporary leave of absence. I've never met him, and since I'm doing him a favor by taking over his column, I don't know why he would possibly have a grudge against me, but Al said he should be checked out, because you never know what someone else is thinking. The next one I wrote down is Jessica Simmons. Come to think of it, you might know her."

DeeDee made a face. "I remember the name. If it's who I'm thinking of, her daughter went to high school with Tink and Briana. Is that the one? And as I remember she had a pretty sharp tongue."

"Yes, that's the one. I ran into her a couple of weeks ago. It's a long shot, but something about how she was that day gave me the impression she really doesn't like me." Cassie grimaced. "I'm not sure what I've done to upset her, but I sure got that feeling from talking with her."

"I can't imagine you upsetting anyone," DeeDee said, confused. "Exactly what happened?"

"I'd just parked in a downtown parking garage, and she drove in behind me. I was glad to see her, since she writes a food blog, which I think is quite good. I'm sure you've heard of it, A Gourmand's Guide to Eats. Anyway, I wanted to ask her if she'd like to team up with me on some restaurant reviews. That way, we could cross-promote each other. I could reach her readers, and she could reach mine. I thought it was a great idea, but she said she was in a hurry and had to go."

"Yes," DeeDee said. "I know the blog you mean. I've used some of her recipes for Deelish. I thought some were good, and some not so good, but why does that make her a possible suspect?"

Cassie thought for a second or two. "Well, as we talked, she became more and more agitated. I realized I was probably keeping her from a meeting or something, so I apologized and asked if she wanted to get together so we could talk about it when she had more time. Not only did she turn me down flat and rush off in a rage, but something weird happened when I got back to my car a little later."

"What happened?"

"The paint on both sides of my Mercedes was badly scratched. The scratches were pretty deep, and it looked to me like it had been done deliberately, probably with a key. I looked around at the other cars parked near mine, but none of them seemed to have been damaged, and there were plenty that were a lot nicer than mine."

DeeDee looked over at Balto, who was standing by the front door. "No walkies till later, Balto. Al and Jake will be back soon." Balto whined, and laid down next to the door. "I'd agree with you. I definitely think Jessica is worth following up on," she said to Cassie. "Who was the last one?"

"Someone else you might know. Do you remember Nora Jenkins, the woman from the Seattle Art Museum?"

DeeDee laughed. "As if I could ever forget her. She was a real battle-ax." DeeDee had encountered Nora when she'd volunteered as a docent at the Seattle Art Museum before she moved to Bainbridge Island. Cassie had previously been on the leadership team at the museum and worked closely with Nora, who was a conservator, before Nora had retired a couple of years earlier.

Nora's run-ins with management were legendary, and one incident ended with the police being called after Nora held a knife to a priceless painting and threatened to ruin it unless Cassie agreed to review her salary package with the Director of Human Resources. "I thought she moved out of state."

Cassie shrugged. "So did I, but for some reason, I remembered the last words she said to me when she was leaving the museum."

"Which were?"

"She was upset about going, and I encouraged her to look forward to her future and enjoy her retirement. She turned to me, and sneered, 'Cassie, you don't know what your future holds. You better keep looking over your shoulder. You never know when trouble might strike your perfect life.'"

DeeDee scribbled all three of the names on her notepad. "What a charming person," she said in a sarcastic voice. "When Al and Jake get back we can find out if Rob's come up with anything yet. He's usually pretty quick to get information. "Since we're kind of at loose ends, how about a game of Scrabble?"

Cassie said, "Fine. But let me warn you, I'm good."

DeeDee shrugged. "You may be, but remember, I've got a gun." She looked up to see Cassie's face break into a broad smile, and went to find the Scrabble board.

CHAPTER SEVEN

Jessica Simmons checked her website stats and frowned. "Good grief, this is not good," she muttered to herself, straightening her glasses and refreshing the page, hoping to see better numbers.

Her Google Analytics account was telling her that the traffic for her food and restaurant review blog, A Gourmand's Guide to Good Eats, was down for the third month in a row. Worse than that, with only a few days left in the month, the blog's page views for March were coming out below the threshold for one of her main sponsors, a Seattle food delivery service that paid for banner ads on her site. They'd already called her earlier in the month checking to see if there were any technical problems, since the ad click-through rate they tracked to orders on their site had fallen drastically.

Now, she knew the reason why. It was very simple. There was practically no traffic to send their way. If things didn't pick up within another couple of weeks, Jessica could expect a call from them cancelling the ads, and with them, her main source of income.

She lifted her mug of coffee to her lips and grimaced when the cold, gritty liquid hit her tongue. She stood up from the rickety wooden chair in front of her laptop computer and walked across the cracked linoleum floor of her studio apartment to the microwave in the corner. She put the half-full cup of coffee inside and pressed the start button. Heating it for thirty seconds, she raised it to her mouth again, her heart sinking as she looked around at her dismal surroundings.

Her office space consisted of a desk against one wall where her ancient laptop was perched. She had to keep it connected to the power socket at all times, since the battery had died a long time ago. There was a narrow space between the desk and her bed, which lined another wall, with just enough room for bookshelves at the end of the bed that had a small TV screen on top of it. The television wasn't hooked up to a cable service, just a USB device plugged in the back that was connected to the internet and allowed Jessica to watch Netflix.

Jessica shared the Netflix account with her daughter Ashley, who lived nearby with her deadbeat boyfriend, Jackson. Her Netflix membership level only allowed one viewer at a time, so most of the time Jessica was out of luck if she wanted to watch anything. Jackson was out of work and hogged the account access, bingeing on Netflix most of his waking hours.

The rest of the tiny apartment was taken up with a green, oversized velvet sofa which was comfortable, but had clearly seen better days, and a coffee table where Jessica ate her meals. The kitchen, if you could call it that, consisted of a length of laminate countertop which housed the microwave oven, an electric cooktop, and a sink.

Under the counter was one storage cupboard, a silverware drawer with a fake door underneath, and a refrigerator. The bathroom, such as it was, was behind a curtain by the bookshelves. Pretty much everything Jessica owned fit inside that one twelve-by-fifteen studio apartment, and she hated every inch of it.

There was a knock on the door, and she turned around to open it. Her daughter Ashley dropped by most mornings on the way to her part-time job in a laundromat.

"Good morning, Mom," Ashley said, pushing past her and slumping onto the sofa. "Do you have any laundry you want me to take care of? I can do it for you and drop it off on my way home this afternoon."

Jessica put her cup down on the coffee table and folded her arms. "I don't know why you work in that place. If you'd concentrated on your studies at school like I told you, instead of running around with good-for-nothings like that Jackson fellow, maybe you'd have some sort of a respectable job by now."

Ashley raised an eyebrow. "You mean like you? Please, don't take this the wrong way, Mom, but you're kind of old to be a startup entrepreneur. Why don't you leave that to Mark Zuckerberg? The sooner you admit you're out of your depth with an online business and go back to cooking in cafes, the better it will be for everyone. Then, maybe you'd relax a little."

Jessica raised her hand and began shaking her finger at Ashley. "Listen to me, young lady. Show some respect for your mother for a change. That pig of a father of yours left us with nothing, and I've cooked and cleaned for years to make ends meet. I did everything I could for you, didn't I?"

Without giving Ashley a chance to reply, she continued to rant. "Now that it's time to do something for me, how are you repaying me? For sure it's not by being supportive, oh no. My website's just one more thing that you can use to make fun of me. I suppose you think it's pretty funny that my business is ruined? And it's all because of that meddling mother of that friend of yours. I bet you two just can't stop laughing at me."

Ashley's eyes widened, and she shook her head. "Mom, I have no idea what you're talking about. Who on earth do you mean?"

"Briana Roberts, that's who." Jessica said, laughing hollowly. "You know, your teenage partner in crime. Ever since her mother took over as the Food Spy in The Seattle Times, my blog rankings have tanked. It seems like there's a new local food hero in town, and it's not me. The latest comments on the blog are scathing, let me see...I'll read some to you."

Jessica strode over to her laptop and clicked the keyboard, causing the screen to awaken from sleep mode. "Oh yes, here we go. 'Cassie Roberts has a tongue-in-cheek way of bringing food to life, whether she likes what's on the menu or not. The author of the Gourmand Guide to Eats blog could learn a thing or two from Cassie's knack for down-to earth food reviews served with a delicious dollop of real life.' Or, how about this one… 'Boring blog. Let's have more spice from the Gourmand and less of the nicey nice.'"

Ashley looked up at her mother, her face solemn. "Mom, if you're going to put yourself online, you've got to have a thick skin. Don't take it personally. For what it's worth, I think those comments are pure gold. Give readers what they want. Why not ruffle a few feathers, and tell it like it is? If some place you're reviewing sucks, don't be afraid to say it loud and clear."

"But what about the advertisers?" Jessica asked, jutting her chin out. "If I don't keep them happy, I won't have any income."

"Mom, in case you didn't know, you're supposed to be impartial," Ashley said with a sigh. "And it kind of goes without saying that if you don't have any readers, you won't have any income either. I haven't read Cassie's column, nor have I spoken to Briana in ages, but I'm sure if I asked her, she could get her mom to call you with some tips for your column."

Jessica's voice reached a high-pitched shriek. "Don't you dare, missy. I never cared for that smug Roberts family and right now, I care for them even less. They were nothing but flashy cars and fancy houses. I don't think any of them ever did an honest day's work in their life. And what you just said is so typical of you, stabbing me in the back every chance you get. I'm finished with you, Ashley, so get out of here, and don't bother coming back."

Her daughter stood up, and said in a pleading voice, "Mom, you're taking this the wrong way. That's not what I meant. I'd help you myself, if I knew how, but I don't know anything about cooking or restaurants. The internet's a big place, and there must be loads of opportunities you haven't even thought of. There's nothing wrong with asking friends for help. I'm sure Briana and Cassie would be more than happy to swap ideas with you."

Jessica held the door open. "OUT. All you do is take, take, take, and cause me nothing but worry. And you, of all people, have the nerve to come around here and criticize me? Why don't you look closer to home? For starters, how about that sleazeball of a boyfriend you have, and what type of sad, hopeless future you'll have with a loser like him. That's not much to look forward to, is it?"

She stood back while Ashley squeezed past, her head and shoulders slumped down. For a moment Jessica felt a twang of remorse at upsetting Ashley, but something inside her made her want to push the knife in, and hurt her even further. "Don't forget to send Jackson my regards. "Oh, I forgot, you'll be working all day while he's lounging at home, eating the food you bought, in the apartment you pay the rent on, right?"

Ashley looked up at her with tears in her eyes, and still Jessica continued. "Oh yeah, I forgot. I guess he'll be watching movies on my Netflix subscription which I'll be canceling today. If you want to do one positive thing for yourself, Ashley, kick that deadbeat out before he drags you down with him. Goodness knows, I'm living proof of how a man can ruin your life."

"Goodbye, Mom," Ashley said as she left her mother's apartment. She walked down the hallway, her hand raised to her eyes to wipe away the tears that kept coming.

Jessica slammed the door with a bang. She hated how Ashley did that pathetic puppy dog act of looking sorry for herself every time Jessica told her the truth about Jackson. Ashley's father, Pat, had been just like Jackson when Jessica had been married to him. Why she'd put up with him until Ashley was ten, she'd never know. The only times Jessica saw Pat now was when she wanted something. Usually it was to ask to use the kitchen at his business premises to try out recipes for her blog, since the cooking facilities in her apartment were so limited. Pat was always agreeable to her requests, and he was even friendly when they did meet. Jessica suspected he'd never gotten over her, and probably still hoped they could get back together, but in her opinion, he was sad, delusional, and weak. It was no surprise that Ashley was just like him, and Jessica despised them both.

She walked the couple of steps back to her desk and stared at the laptop screen. Jessica winced when she read the blog comments again. When she'd started the blog a year earlier, it had taken off through word of mouth, thanks to a couple of local radio interviews. As a result, Jessica had restaurants calling her to ask for reviews, some with offers of payment or free meals in return for favorable reviews. Back then, Jessica didn't know there were Federal Trade Commission rules about disclosure of endorsements or advertisements online. She thought since it was her blog she could write whatever she wanted, and if she'd been paid to write it, it was nobody's business but her own.

When she found out that wasn't the case, she realized her previous business model was unsustainable, and she had to start writing independent reviews which just happened to coincide with the time Cassie had started her Food Spy column in The Seattle Times. As far as Jessica was concerned, it wasn't bad luck, bad timing, or anything she'd done. The decline of A Gourmand's Guide to Eats was all because of one thing, Cassie Roberts, and the unfair push her column had been given by The Seattle Times when it launched.

As a result, three months later Jessica's business was about to collapse. The time to save it was rapidly running out, and there was only one solution Jessica could think of. She'd been running it through her mind for days, and she kept coming back to the same answer.

Bye-bye Food Spy, she thought to herself, *and so long Cassie Roberts. Your fifteen minutes of fame is about to end.*

CHAPTER EIGHT

Jules Moreau whistled to himself as he checked his reflection in the full-length bedroom mirror. He sucked in his stomach and smoothed down his dress shirt, reaching up to fix his fat bow-tie. Pulling it out at either end, his adjustments took some time as he painstakingly made sure the edges were straight and symmetrical. He'd been diagnosed with Obsessive Compulsive Disorder as a child after a manic episode involving a muddy kitten, a scrub brush, and a bottle of bleach.

Jules had turned the scrub brush and the bleach on himself after the dirty kitten had jumped up on him, and his arms still had the scars to prove it. The kitten, Frisky, wasn't hurt, although she definitely hadn't appreciated Jules' attempts to dunk her in a bathtub filled with steaming hot water and his mother's scented bubble bath. Frisky escaped from Jules' clutches and jumped out the bathroom window, taking refuge in a neighbor's garden where she was eventually found, cowering behind a flowerpot, by a search-party of eight-year-olds.

Looking good, Jules, he thought to himself, turning sideways to admire the view. Despite the paunch, which was an occupational hazard for a restaurateur, he considered himself to be in good shape for his age, which had been stuck at forty-nine for at least five years. His swarthy looks and dark hair had often drawn comparisons to Johnny Depp, although in Jules' own opinion, he was aging far better than Johnny. He licked his finger and smoothed each of his eyebrows.

"Jules, if you don't hurry up, the awards ceremony will be over." His wife's shrill voice brought him out of his mental movie and back to reality. He pulled on his tuxedo jacket, grabbed the car keys off his dresser, and headed downstairs.

If Sheila Moreau thought he was looking good, she didn't bother to mention it. She was his second wife, and had given him the children his first wife had been unable to produce, but any romantic affection he'd once had for her had left long ago. He was far too much in love with himself to share that with anyone else, so he and Sheila lived separate but amicable lives. Since their children had left home, Jules spent six days a week at his restaurant, Frogities, and Sheila spent his money on spa trips and clothes. The arrangement suited them both.

"You look stunning, *ma cherie*," Jules said, kissing Sheila on the cheek. He always made a point of complimenting his wife on her appearance, even though she rarely returned the favor. As arm candy, she never let him down. Her poker-straight, black, chin-length hair with bangs, contrasted against her pale complexion and blue eyes, and her shimmering silver gown caught the light in all the right places, accentuating her curves.

In the car, Jules cleared his throat. "I need to run this speech past you. Tell me what you think, okay?"

Sheila regarded him with a quizzical smile. "Isn't that a little premature? We don't even know who is going to win the Restaurant of the Year award, unless there's something you haven't told me. And if I'd known it was going to be you, I would have brought my camera."

Jules smiled. "Sheila, you know modesty isn't my strong point, but I do think this is our year. Frogities has been the runner-up too many times for it not to be our turn at the podium. All the improvements we've made over the past year speak for themselves. Think about it—

a Michelin-starred chef, the outdoor terrace, and the rave reviews by all the critics. That's about as good as it gets."

"You could be right," Sheila said, thinking it over. "That new Food Spy in The Seattle Times wrote a great review of your restaurant, and she's pretty tough to please, from what I understand. Okay, shoot. What have you got?"

Jules straightened his face, and glanced at himself in the rear view mirror. "I thought I'd start off with something like... 'Ladies and Gentlemen, I'm speechless with surprise. Please, allow me a moment...' And then, I'll bow my head and sniff, like I'm all choked up."

Sheila chuckled. "You're such a drama king, Jules. They'll see right through it, but do go on."

Jules glared at her. "Then, I'll say I'm honored and humbled to have been chosen from such an esteemed shortlist. Oh, and of course I'll compliment the losers for being so wonderful."

Sheila rolled her eyes. "It's going to kill you to have to say nice things about Le Bijou Bistro. I mean, you might choke on your words, and that would be pretty embarrassing."

"Funny," Jules said as he turned the car onto the Seattle waterfront. "They'll know it's all baloney, of course, but everyone will smile and nod and play along. Le Bijou Bistro gave Frogities a shout-out last year when it won the category, even though Frogities is their main competitor."

"I'd say more of an arch-enemy." Sheila paused as the car slowed down for the line of traffic that was using valet parking at the luxury Edgewater Hotel. "Still, it was the least Bertrand from Le Bijou Bistro could do, since he must have known how close it was. I hope he's as gracious a loser as you were last year, when your name's announced as the winner."

Jules' jaw tightened. He didn't like being reminded of his

humiliation the previous year. He'd been so certain he'd be taking home the Restaurant of the Year plaque engraved with Frogities' name on it, he'd jumped up when the winner of the award was announced, not realizing for a moment that it wasn't him. He'd been very quick thinking when he'd corrected the mistake by giving Bertrand Christolhomme a standing ovation when his nemesis had walked up to the stage. How Jules had contained the rage that consumed him that night, he'd never know. Despite his smiles for the cameras, inside he was plotting revenge. And tonight, his moment would come.

"Good evening, sir," the valet said, greeting him through the open car window. Jules opened his car door and handed the keys to the valet as he stepped out of the car. He linked his arm through Sheila's and smiled at his peers as they entered the lobby of the hotel, only too aware of what a striking couple he and his wife made. Jules always wanted to be the center of attention, and to be ignored was one of his pet peeves.

Once inside the hotel, they made their way to the cocktail reception in The Olympic Room, named for its commanding view of the mountain range in the distance.

"Be nice," Sheila hissed at him through gritted teeth, as she lifted a glass of champagne.

"I am," Jules hissed back. "Stop smiling like that. It looks like your grin is painted on."

Sipping champagne and mingling with the other restaurant owners who he privately considered to be beneath him didn't require much effort on his part. His superiority complex told him they were lucky he'd even talked to them.

"Smug alert," Sheila whispered, when they were alone for a moment.

Jules looked around, surprised. "Where?"

She sighed in an exaggerated manner. "You, Jules. You are being a pain in the you-know-what. Please try and remember not everyone thinks you're as wonderful as you do. Have the class to show at least a little modesty."

Jules shrugged. "I see no reason to hide my light under a bush, or whatever the saying is. These people will soon be witnessing history in the making. Tonight may be the first award for Frogties, but it won't be the last. And that's a promise."

"What is?" A slim man with a mustache said as he stepped up beside them. "Sheila, my dear. May I say how ravishing you look tonight?"

Sheila raised her glass to the man and smiled.

Jules eyed him with disdain. "Ah, Bertrand," he smirked. "I was just saying to Sheila that this evening will be a night we won't forget for a long time. I see you're sweating. I'm not surprised. I would be too, if I were you."

Bertrand wiped his brow. "I see you're as charming as ever, Jules. It's just as well I'm so good-natured, or I might take offense. There's nothing keeping me awake at night, except perhaps the pending visit from The Food Spy next Wednesday, but you, on the other hand, look as though you could do with a good eight hours of sleep."

Sheila giggled behind her glass, only looking away when Jules stared her down.

"How nice of The Food Spy to warn you she's coming. I guess you need all the advance notice you can get. She loved Frogties, of course. As a matter of fact, she couldn't fault it."

Bertrand beamed. "I read the write-up, and that she did, but let's wait and see what she has to say about Le Bijou Bistro. Since it's her birthday, we're planning on making sure it goes off flawlessly." He winked at Jules. "Now, if you'll excuse me, I have an award to win." He sauntered off, turning his back to an open-mouthed Jules.

"Come on, Jules, let's go to our table," Sheila said, setting down her glass. "Ignore him. It was just a bit of harmless chitchat. Right?"

Jules grunted and followed Sheila to the table. He still had three courses to endure before his moment of truth, made even more painful by the need to pretend to enjoy the company of the other restaurant owners who were seated at their table and with whom he had no interest in talking to. It was even worse listening to their boring stories.

While the entree of maple glazed duck breast turned out to be delicious, the conversation was not. He was grateful Sheila was a natural mixer at these types of events. She made small talk and laughed along with the best of them, including Jules, asking nothing of him but a nod when she asked, "Isn't that right, honey?"

It was after 10:00 p.m. when the award ceremony started and more than an hour later when the final award, Restaurant of The Year, was announced. Even though he had his speech written out on a piece of paper in his pocket, and had checked several times to make sure that it was still there, Jules knew it by heart, and was running through it in his head. He'd rehearsed it many times in the mirror at home, right down to the facial expressions, including a couple of moody poses he'd picked up from watching Johnny Depp movies. It wasn't the first time Jules wondered if Johnny would be available in the future to star in the movie of Jules' life, the best of which he was confident was yet to come.

What happened next was such a shock that afterwards, Jules could only remember it as a series of flashbacks. The look on Sheila's face when the winner was called…a roar of applause…so many eyes on him, then looking away…a tall, slim man with a mustache walking up to the stage…laughter as the man on the stage called Jules' name, while holding the award high in the air in triumph.

Jules clutched his head, feeling the onset of a migraine that he knew would last several days. His vision was blurred, the rush in his ears distorting the cacophony of sounds that were bombarding him from all directions. He wanted to cover his ears and run out of there, but that was impossible. He forced himself to clap, and smile, and even raise a glass for Le Bijou Bistro, who took home the top prize of the night. And he vowed right then and there that one way or the other, he would bring that restaurant down once and for all.

The bad publicity his competitor would endure from the death of a patron would be insurmountable, and probably result in it being closed down. And who better to kill than a high-profile diner, the foodie darling of the moment, Cassie Roberts? Bertrand had said himself she would be dining at Le Bijou Bistro on Wednesday of next week.

As far as Jules was concerned, it would be her last supper. He hoped she enjoyed it. Too bad she wouldn't be around to write about it.

CHAPTER NINE

It was shortly before noon when Jake and Al arrived at Le Bijou Bistro. Al didn't want to go up on the passenger deck during the ferry crossing from Bainbridge Island, and Jake didn't push it. DeeDee had mentioned to him once that she thought Al didn't seem comfortable on the ferry, and if he had some kind of problem with it, Jake didn't want to embarrass him. Instead, they spent the ride over to Seattle sitting in the car talking about the Seahawks, and the new players who would be playing for them in the fall.

Jake called Rob a couple of times to see if his assistant had any news for them yet, but he wasn't able to get connected. The cell phone signal was intermittent on the ferry, and the chances of having a telephone conversation without it breaking up were slim to none. He decided to call him again when they reached Seattle.

"Ima gonna' park here," Al said, slowing his Maserati Levante and pulling into a no parking zone near the restaurant. "We ain't got no time to waste."

"You good for the parking ticket coming your way, Al?"

Al grinned. "That's how I roll, Jake. Why don'tcha take a look in the glove compartment?"

Jake opened the glove compartment, and an avalanche of parking tickets fell out. Jake scratched his head. "Interesting," he muttered, stuffing them back in. It seemed as though Al liked to live dangerously in everything he did. Jake didn't want to point out that four or more unpaid parking tickets would result in the car getting the Scofflaw Boot, which was a wheel locking device that immobilized vehicles until all of the outstanding tickets had been paid, along with an additional fine of $145.

Al must have been reading his mind. "Frienda' mine works for the city. Let's jes' leave it at that, okay?"

Jake turned to him with a blank look on his face. "What was that you were saying? Don't think I caught it, Al."

Al was already climbing out of the car. "Yer' learnin' Jake. C'mon, let's go."

Jake caught up to where Al was striding down the street toward the dark red painted exterior of the restaurant on the corner where they'd dined the previous evening. Al banged on the door, which was locked from the inside, although they could see the staff through the windows.

"Open up," he bellowed, while his fist continued to rattle the door.

Inside Le Bijou Bistro, several heads turned, and a man approached the entrance dressed in a black waistcoat and pants, with a white shirt and black bow-tie. His shirt sleeves were rolled up, and he was carrying a clipboard. Jake recognized him as the *maitre'd* from the night before.

"We open at midday, sir," The *maitre'd* said through the door, making no attempt to open it. He pointed to the sign hanging against the glass. "Please, come back then."

Al clasped his hands together, stretching out his arms until his fingers made a loud, sharp click. Jake saw the *maitre'd* wince, indicating that the sound had also reached him. Al's voice was low and menacing. "Ima gonna' ask you again, sir, to please open the door. This is matter of grave urgency."

Al reached inside his jacket, and Jake held his breath while he waited for Al to produce his gun. It wasn't something Jake would have recommended in broad daylight, and he looked around to see if anyone else had noticed them. The only other people in the street were quickly walking to wherever they were going, minding their own business, and not paying any attention to Al and Jake. Jake exhaled a sigh of relief when instead of a weapon, Al produced a wad of cash, which he held up for a moment before the *maitre'd* stepped closer, turned the lock of the door, and held it open for them.

"*Monsieurs*, please come in."

Al went in first, pressing the cash into the man's hand, followed by Jake. The *maitre'd* secreted the cash with a sleight of hand that came from years of accepting discreet tips. He could not have been more charming as he lifted two menus, and beckoned them to follow him. "Please, this way, gentlemen," he said, heading for a table by the window.

"Keep walkin'," Al instructed him, "down towards the back, outta view from people goin' by." They walked the length of the bar, where the bartender stood polishing glasses in anticipation of a busy lunch crowd, and then past several waiters setting tables with gleaming silverware. When they reached the back corner near the kitchen, Al spoke again. "Sit," he ordered them both. Al sat beside the *maitre'd*, and Jake sat opposite them. Al's back was to the wall, giving him a clear view of the empty restaurant. He removed his sunglasses, folding them carefully on the table, and squinted at the *maitre'd*. "What's yer' name?"

"Pierre, sir," the man replied. He held out two menus, and his voice cracked. "Will you be eating with us today?"

Jake shook his head, and reached for the menus, setting them down. The cooking aromas of the dishes being prepared in the kitchen were tempting, but the only thing on his and Al's menu was solving Megan Reilly's murder. "We were hoping to ask you a few questions, Pierre," Jake began, "about the incident at the restaurant last night. My friend here is concerned that the woman who was murdered was sitting at the table originally reserved for his wife and him. Understandably, that causes him a great deal of distress."

Pierre shrugged his shoulders and raised his palms in the air. "I know nothing of any murder, *monsieur*. It was a very sad case of a woman who choked on her food. It happens rarely, but we are not the only restaurant where such a tragedy has occurred. Our sympathies are with the family, but I assure you there was no foul play involved at Le Bijou Bistro last night."

Al cracked his knuckles which immediately commanded Pierre's attention. Then he began to move his jaw from side to side, the sound of his teeth grinding making Pierre shrink back. "Why don'tcha think a little harder, Pierre? When we was leavin', I overheard the waiters whisperin' in French somethin' 'bout a murder. Ima pretty good *à la Française*, you see." Al looked over at Jake and winked. "Remind me to tell ya 'bout my stint in the French Foreign Legion some time."

Al and Jake both turned to Pierre, who was shifting uncomfortably in his seat. "Take yer' time, Pierre," Al said, folding his arms. "We ain't goin' nowhere. We got all day. But here's a tip from Uncle Al. Why don'tcha jes' get it off yer' chest, and we'll be outta' yer' way? I guess ya'll have customers arrivin' fer lunch soon. Yer' call, my friend."

Jake admired how relaxed Al was in this kind of situation. He was speaking to Pierre as casually as if he were inquiring about the price of apples at Whole Foods Market. Not for the first time, Jake wondered about the pace of Al's previous life in the Mafia. It must have been frenetic if a conversation like this didn't cause him to skip a beat.

Pierre sighed heavily. His voice was low when he began talking. "I know nothing for sure. Only that a cake was delivered yesterday afternoon with instructions it was to be a surprise for the couple dining at Table 12. The person who delivered it was insistent it should be served to both diners for dessert, even if they ordered something else."

Al frowned. "Both diners, ya' say? Did the man at Table 12, Mr. Robertson I think was his name, also have some of the cake?"

"*Non, monsieur.*" Pierre's head moved from side to side. "When the cake was served, the man said he wasn't big on chocolate, but the lady accepted. A waiter who was taking an order at the next table witnessed the whole thing. He told me he didn't think the lady choked. The way he described it to me, it was more like she couldn't breathe and went into a seizure after a couple of bites."

"Let me see if I've got this right," Jake said. "You said the cake wasn't made here, and that it was delivered from somewhere else. Is that right?"

"*Oui, monsieur.*"

Al drummed his fingers on the table. "Let's cut to the chase. Where did the cake come from, and what sorta' joint accepts random cake deliveries with instructions who they should go to, without checkin'?"

Pierre looked haughtily at Al and said, "*Monsieur,* we are not the cake police. It happens quite often that a special cake is delivered for a customer. The supplier was one of our regulars, a reputable local company called Creative Cakes. I understand it was a new delivery driver, but that is not so unusual either. Mr. Robertson and his companion were also celebrating a special event last night, so it was an innocent mistake."

"They ain't celebratin' now," Al said, his face grim. "That poor Robertson guy must be goin' out of his mind." He turned to Jake. "We gotta' find him, and tell him we're gonna' help get to the bottom of this."

"I'm already working on that," Jake confirmed. "I have his

telephone number, and I'm planning on calling him later. Pierre, you've been a big help, thank you. Is there anything else you think we should know?"

"Know about what?" A tall, slim man with a mustache appeared at the end of the table. He nodded at Pierre. "That will be all, Pierre. I'm sure you have work to do."

Pierre excused himself and rose from the table, hurrying off.

"Gentlemen. My name is Bertrand Christolhomme. I'm the owner of Le Bijou Bistro. How may I help you?"

Jake extended his hand. "Jake Rogers. I'm a private investigator helping with the investigation into the death of Megan Reilly, the woman who died here last night." He motioned to Al, who was eyeing Bertrand. "This is a friend of mine, Al De Duco. It's possible Al and his wife were the intended victims."

Bertrand's eyes narrowed. "Are you sure no one else sent you?" He shook hands with Jake and Al in turn, before slumping into the seat Pierre had vacated.

Al grunted. "Sure we're sure. Who else d'ya think mighta' sent us?"

"It's probably just me being paranoid," Bertrand said, looking around to see if anyone could hear him. "This incident is going to cost me dearly. There's already been a leak saying the coroner's preliminary findings are that the woman was poisoned. You can imagine what terrible publicity that is for my business. The phone hasn't stopped ringing with cancellations all morning. I thought that weasel Moreau might have sent you, looking for more dirt so he can leak it to the press. He's going to be milking this to his advantage, I have no doubt of that."

"Do you mean Jules Moreau?" Jake said. "The guy who owns Frogties? I saw the Food Spy review of his place a while back in The Seattle Times. There was a quote from him saying he was expecting to win the Restaurant of the Year award. The reason I remembered it was because it seemed like a very arrogant thing to say. In fact, it made me never want to go there."

Bertrand smiled tightly. "Yes, that's him. I saw him last week at The Edgewater, when Le Bijou Bistro picked up the very award he thought Frogities would be taking home. He acted like he was gracious in defeat, but believe me, I know he's out to even the score. He's already poached my best wait staff and chefs. If there's any way he can use this to twist the knife in more, he will. He won't rest until my restaurant is closed down, and I'm bankrupt."

Al exchanged a look with Jake. "Ya' think he hates ya' enough to murder someone in yer' restaurant so as to discredit it?"

Bertrand rubbed his unshaven chin. "It's hard to imagine anyone's mind works that way, but yes, I guess it's possible."

Al stood up, and Jake followed his lead. Al slapped Bertrand on the back. "Thanks fer your help, *monsieur*. Ima thinkin' we need to pay Mr. Moreau a little visit."

They nodded at Pierre on the way out, who didn't make eye contact with either of them.

When they were outside, Al turned to Jake and said, "Yer' thinkin' what I'm thinkin,' right?"

Jake nodded. "Yep. Let's add Moreau to the list of suspects. I'll cover him and Creative Cakes. How about you call Rob and see about the others?"

Al walked rapidly towards his car. "Got it. Let's make sure our ladies are safe first. Coupla' other people I need to check on as well. Looks like whoever sent that cake was quite happy to kill both me an' Cassie. I gotta' call Harry, for protection."

"Who's Harry?"

"An ol' buddy of mine," Al said. "Full name's Harry the Hatchet."

Jake wished he hadn't' asked.

"One more thing, Jake. It jes' occurred to me that Cassie wrote in one of her columns that she always asked to be seated at Table No. 12 when she visited a restaurant, cuz' she's been told that's where the restaurant seats 'portant guests. I overheard her request Table No. 12 when she made the reservations at Le Bijou Bistro."

"Al, that's doesn't sound good."

"I know."

CHAPTER TEN

Al stared at the view across Elliott Bay and Puget Sound from Cassie and his penthouse suite at The Four Seasons Hotel. Apart from the occasional spider in the bathtub, he couldn't fault the place, but he was definitely looking forward to when the home they'd bought on Bainbridge Island would be ready for them to move in. The bullet-proof windows and state-of-the-art security system were going to be installed shortly, and the moving company was on standby.

Cassie had talked a lot about buying a sailboat, but so far, Al had been able to stall her. Before that happened, he had to get over his fear of water, or it would be like throwing money down the drain. Given the way he felt right now, there was no way he'd get on a small sailboat. He could live with an expanse of water at the end of his new garden, but going on a boat for fun was beyond his comprehension, and it wasn't even for fishing.

Since it meant so much to Cassie, he'd agreed to her suggestion to attend a series of hypnotherapy sessions for his aquaphobia. Privately, he thought some of Cassie's ideas about new-age therapies were just a bunch of mumbo-jumbo, and he suspected the hypnotherapist was bound to be an overpriced quack. But feeling about Cassie as he did, if she asked him to jump off a mountain without a parachute in a leap of faith, he knew he'd do it. However, he'd made her promise she wouldn't start waving healing crystals around. That was where he drew the line.

Al just wanted to find out who had murdered Megan Reilly, so he could eliminate whoever was gunning for him and Cassie, if in fact someone was, and get on with what he was hoping would be a long and happy married life. If the last few months since he'd met Cassie were any indication, they had a rosy future ahead.

He pressed in Rob's number on his phone. "Yo Rob, it's Al De Duco. Whaddya' got fer me?"

"Hey, Al, good to hear from you. I've been waiting for your call. I've got some pretty interesting stuff."

Al paced up and down by the windows, impatient for Rob to get to the point. "Shoot, man, and don't leave nothin' out."

"I won't," Rob began. "First off, as to the restaurants Cassie wrote about, you know, the ones that she gave bad reviews to in her Food Spy column."

"Yeah?"

"They all say business has never been better. It appears there's truth in the old saying that there's no such thing as bad publicity. All of them are reporting an upturn in reservations since Cassie reviewed them. They're calling it The Food Spy Factor."

Al grunted. "Even the place where the Seafood Surprise was frozen in the middle? I'm tellin' ya' we didn't expect that. They're lucky Cassie didn't get sick after eating there, or I woulda'...er, I dunno', I woulda' hadda' take some serious action."

"Knowing you, Al," Rob said, "I would expect nothing less. Here's what I found out. When a restaurant gets a bad review, the regulars often band together to defend the place they love. They get up in arms about it on social media, and before you know it, the restaurant's Trip Advisor profile has gone viral. The proprietors post clever retorts about the review's shortcomings or the fact that the reviewer didn't tip, and then they grab the headlines."

Al wasn't sure what social media was, or if the Trip Advisor was a real person. He scratched his head. "Rob, ya' lost me, man. Is this something to do with that iPad thing Cassie keeps tappin' on? All that tappin' and swipin'. . .makes my head spin." He lowered his voice, in case Cassie could hear. "One time, I heard her talkin' to some weird woman called Siri. Is that normal?"

There was a pause, while Rob considered his answer. He decided it was a good thing they weren't on Face Time. The last thing he wanted was for Al to see the grin he was wearing. "Um, yes. In fact, it's entirely normal and nothing to worry about at all. Another thing—because Food Spy always has something good to say about a place, however minor, people are visiting those establishments to see the cute waiter, or taste a secret recipe like Kale Explosion Juice, that sort of thing."

"Stop right there. I understand Cassie's obsession for kale, but what cute waiter are ya' talkin' bout?"

"Al, I'm not sure I—"

"Spit it out, Rob. Or Ima gonna' have to kill ya'."

"Al, I sincerely hope you don't mean that," Rob sighed. "But for what it's worth, here goes. In one of the reviews, Cassie mentioned a handsome waiter who flirted with her. She said if she'd been twenty years younger, and not already dating an even more handsome man of a more suitable age, she might have written her number on the check like he asked."

"Huh," Al said, a slow smile spreading across his face. "That's all right then. But Ima gonna' tell Cassie she gotta' stop being so nice in them places. Gonna' get her in trouble. Anyways, sounds like ya' don't think we need to worry 'bout any of them restaurants, is that right?"

"That's about it," Rob said. "The next person of interest is easy to rule out too. Nora Jenkins, the woman who worked with Cassie at the museum?"

"Go on," Al said. "Don't tell me she ran off with the cute waiter? I really gotta' meet this guy."

"Nope, she died over a year ago. Spent the first year of her retirement traveling the world, only to be run over by a bus on her return to Seattle. She was killed instantly. It's kind of ironic."

Al sat on the sofa, kicked off his shoes, and put his feet on the coffee table. "Yeah, that's too bad. I think that's what Cassie calls karma. Who else ya' got?"

"Myles Lambert, the food critic Cassie's covering for. From what I've learned, he's not at all well-liked at the newspaper. I hear he thinks of himself as some kind of a literary genius, and looks down on the rest of the staff. He's taken time off from his column to write a book, but it's a mass-market foodie travel guide, nothing quite as grand as his aspirations. According to my contact, the other people at the newspaper wouldn't be all that sorry if he didn't come back to it. I did find out it seems that Myles' nose was bent out of joint recently when the Lifestyle Editor suggested he take more time off if he needed it."

"Who's the editor?" Al asked. "Ya' speak to him direct?"

"It's a she," Rob replied. "Gloria Ekenbach. She wouldn't take my calls. I'd suggest you follow up with her in person, if possible. I don't have an in."

"I don't either," Al said, "but Cassie does. Ima gonna see what I can do. That just leaves the Simmons woman, I think. What's the skinny on her?"

Al heard Rob take a deep breath. "Well, where do you want me to start?"

"At the beginnin' would be good. Anything that might make her a murderer."

"Okay, here goes. Jessica Simmons is in her forties and divorced.

She has one child, a daughter named Ashley, who went to school with Cassie's daughter, Briana, and DeeDee's daughter, Tink, which you probably already know. Briana and Ashley were particularly close as teenagers since neither one of them cared all that much about academics. After failing to graduate from high school, Ashley's approval rating with her mother fell even further due to a series of dead-end jobs and deadbeat boyfriends."

"Got it," Al said, "but it's Jessica I'm interested in. What's her beef with Cassie?"

"Jessica runs a food blog that's moderately popular, more so out of luck than any particular skill on her part. She's been working on it for several years, and before she started it she held various positions in the catering industry. She did everything from cooking in cafes, to washing dishes when times were hard, which with her was most of the time. She divorced Ashley's father over ten years ago, and she's been struggling financially ever since. Her food blog is just the latest in a line of failed business ventures."

"I see. So what you're saying is she could be jealous of Cassie's success at The Seattle Times. Would that be right?" Al reached down to scratch his toe.

"I'd be surprised if she wasn't," Rob said. "Also, another parent from the high school told me Jessica always had something bad to say about Cassie, ever since Ashley had sleepovers years ago at Cassie's house on Mercer Island. Seems like Jessica was in awe of Cassie's privileged lifestyle, and never missed a chance to bad-mouth Cassie behind her back to the other parents."

"Ima dislikin' this Jessica Simmons woman more by the minute," Al said.

"I thought that's what you'd say," Rob said. "It may be a coincidence, but there's something else you ought to know."

Al had a feeling come over him that what Rob was going to tell him was going to make him crazy. "Ain't no such thing as a coincidence. Go on."

"Jessica's ex-husband, Pat Simmons, is also the owner of Creative Cakes."

Al swung his feet off the coffee table and sat bolt upright. His feeling had been right. That statement made him really worried. "Does Jake know about this? He's on his way to Creative Cakes this afternoon."

"Yes," Rob confirmed. "I just briefed him about the coincidence."

"All right, thanks Rob," Al said, standing up and stretching. "Ima gonna' leave that to Jake, he's capable of dealin' with it. Yer' help has been above and beyond, as usual. I appreciate it, my man."

"No problem," Rob said. "Call me if you need anything more."

Al turned as Cassie approached the lounge area, with the first smile he'd seen on her face since before Megan Reilly's murder. "I will," Al said as he ended the call and greeted Cassie. "What's made you so happy?"

Cassie held out her phone. "I had a couple of missed calls from Briana while we were out earlier," she beamed. "Maybe she was calling to wish me Happy Birthday."

"Your birthday was yesterday, sweetie pie," Al reminded her, with an affectionate grin.

"Yes, and it's one I won't forget for a long time, but my phone was off all night, so maybe she did try to call me. You know I never switch it on unless I need to call someone. I only saw the calls today when I turned it on to call the newspaper after we got back from DeeDee's."

"Here's the thing, Cassie," Al said. "See, sometimes people might wanna' call ya'. The phone's no darn use to ya' if it's not switched on.

Did Briana leave a voice message?"

Cassie's face was blank. "I never get voice messages. I'm not sure why."

"Here," Al said, reaching out his hand. "Show me yer' phone." Taking Cassie's device, he pressed a few buttons, held the phone up to his ear, and listened. "Yer' voice mail's switched off. Ima gonna reset it now, okay?"

Cassie nodded. "Thanks, Al."

"Why were you callin' the paper?" Al asked.

"To tell them I can't work for a while, like you told me. It's not safe, is it?"

"Not till we get to the bottom of this Megan Reilly murder, it's not. Did ya' speak to Gloria, yer' editor?"

Cassie smiled at him. "Al, you remembered! You've usually got no memory for names. No, she was out of the office, but her personal assistant told me she'll be back tomorrow."

"I think you might wanna' go there and speak to her in person," Al said. "And see what ya' can find out 'bout this Lambert guy. Can ya' get DeeDee to go with ya'?"

"I'm sure I could," Cassie said. "Are you coming too?"

"Nah, think I might scare Gloria off. Frienda' mine, Harry, is gonna' look after ya'. Nice, normal lookin' feller, but he ain't no pussy cat, lemme tell ya'. Speakin' of feline friends, while yer' there Ima gonna' pay a visit to a certain lady who ain't no pushover either."

"Kitten Knight?"

"Yep," Al said, pulling Cassie close. He wouldn't let her out of his sight unless it was absolutely necessary, but there was no way he could take her with him to see Kitten.

There was no telling what Kitten might do.

CHAPTER ELEVEN

Jake waited on the sidewalk in front of the Seattle Waterfront Marriott for a person fitting Luke Robertson's description to pick him up in a red Honda. When he'd called Luke, and introduced himself after leaving Le Bijou Bistro, Luke wanted to meet up with him sooner rather than later so the two of them could go directly to Creative Cakes, which was on the outskirts of the city.

Al had dropped him off at the Marriott on his way back to Bainbridge Island.

A shiny red Honda pulled over to the curb, and the driver leaned across and peered through the window at Jake. He gave Jake a questioning look. The young man was muscular and tan, with short cropped black hair. Jake knew an off-duty police officer when he saw one. As he strode over to the car, Luke pushed the passenger door open for him, and Jake climbed inside.

Jake introduced himself with a handshake. "Jake Rogers. Sorry to meet you in such sad circumstances, Luke." He could see the hurt in the young man's eyes. Luke's jaw was set in a straight expressionless line.

"Thanks for agreeing to meet me, Jake," Luke said, his voice flat. "Dan Hewson, the Chief of Police, speaks highly of you. I understand you're already involved in investigating the Megan Reilly case for other reasons. I just want the person who killed my fiancée brought to justice."

"Your fiancée?" Jake said in surprise. "Forgive me, I didn't realize you and Megan were engaged."

"I proposed last night," Luke said, looking away from Jake. He was staring vacantly ahead through the windshield, at nothing in particular. The car behind them honked its horn, and with a jolt, Luke put the Honda in gear, and they pulled away from the sidewalk. "Megan said yes, and made me the happiest man alive. For all of, oh, fifteen minutes. And then...you know."

Jake looked up from where he was tapping the address for Creative Cakes into the screen on the satellite navigation system on the dashboard. He was at a loss for words.

Luke cleared his throat. "So, where are we headed?"

"Looks like it's not that far from here. We're on the right side of town. Are you sure you're up to this, Luke? It must be very difficult for you right now."

"There's no way I can't be involved," Luke said. "Megan's body is at the morgue, and her parents are there to deal with things when the coroner is done. I'm not family, and never will be now." His voice was void of emotion.

"I'm sensing some animosity there," Jake said. "Are you not on good terms with Megan's family?"

"Oh, they're civil to me," Luke said. "But Bill and Susan never approved of their daughter dating a cop, never mind marrying one. Somehow they think this is all my fault. They can freeze me out of the funeral arrangements all they want, but they can't stop me from doing what I'm good at, seeking justice. And I intend to."

"Glad to hear it," Jake said, in an admiring tone. "Any more news from the coroner's office?"

"The conclusion seems to be that Megan was poisoned with cyanide," Luke said. "It's fast-acting and kills its victim in a matter of minutes. It's also easily available on the internet. I think illegal websites like The Silk Road have a lot to answer for the damage they can cause."

"I couldn't agree more," Jake said. He knew about the darknet markets Luke was referring to. Although the original Silk Road had been shut down and its founder imprisoned for life without parole, it was the forerunner of the current online black market sites dealing in illegal substances and accepting non-traceable payments such as Bitcoin. "The cyanide was in the cake, I take it?"

"Yes," Luke said. "I can't stand chocolate cake, otherwise I'd be dead too. Megan said it was delicious and tried to coax me into taking just a tiny bite of it. She was holding out the cake on her fork, trying to squeeze it in my mouth. I can still see the silly grin on her face." He shook his head. "Maybe if I'd tried a bite of it first and felt sick before Megan had any, I could have saved her life."

"Don't beat yourself up like that," Jake said. "You're here now, and we're going to find her killer. My friend will make sure of that."

"I don't get it," Luke said. "Why is the person you're working with so interested in who killed Megan? What's the connection?"

"Let's just say he has a vested interest," Jake said. He wanted to sound reassuring, without going to details about Al's background. Luke, who was frowning, didn't push the matter. It was obvious he had a lot on his mind.

The satellite navigation system instructed them to turn left into the parking lot of a small commercial building containing six units. Jake thought it was very similar to the set-up DeeDee had on Bainbridge Island for her catering business, Deelish. As well as the sign for Creative Cakes, there was a car valet outfit, a mobile dog groomer with a couple of trucks outside, a home interior showroom, and a beauty supply wholesaler. The last unit had a real estate agent's sign stuck to the closed shuttered doors.

Luke parked in one of the spaces allocated for customer parking, and the two men got out. The door to the Creative Cakes unit led into a small reception area, sparsely decorated with a couple of chairs, worn carpet tiles and various pictures on the walls of spectacular-looking fancy cakes. The one that grabbed Jake's attention was a Disney-inspired Cinderella carriage, perfect in detail right down to the footman and horses. It was taller than the little girl and her friends who were standing beside it, grinning, with the little girl's birthday balloons visible in the background.

No one was at the desk, and the only sound they heard was music coming from the back room. Jake rang a tarnished brass bell on the counter, and he and Luke stood in silence while the bell's jingle was followed by muffled footsteps. A young woman wearing what looked like white hospital scrubs with a pink shower cap on her head, and a pink plastic bootie on each foot covering her shoes, appeared through a door in the back.

"Hi," she said, grinning. "Are you here to pick up an order? What's the number, please?"

Luke spoke up. "No, we're not customers. Is it possible to speak to whoever's in charge?" He flashed his police badge.

The smile faded from the woman's face, and she nodded. "Um, sure. I'll get Pat. Just a moment, please." As an afterthought, she reached under the counter and produced a tray of rainbow-colored cupcakes and set them on top of it. "Help yourselves."

Luke stared at the cupcakes before turning away. Out of respect for Luke, Jake tried to ignore them, although they looked delicious. Fat and succulent, with a thick layer of frosting, each cake was topped with glitter dust and a mini unicorn. *Those are definitely girl cakes*, Jake thought as he looked at the glitter and unicorns, determined to resist. In the end, he had to turn away to stop himself from grabbing one. He had a sweet tooth, as DeeDee could testify.

The door behind the counter opened again and this time a man entered, dressed in normal clothes, except for the clear plastic cap covering his hair and the plastic booties on his feet. He pulled off the cap and threw it in the waste basket in the corner. "I'm Pat Simmons," he said as he looked at Jake and Luke, "the owner of Creative Cakes. I understand you're police officers. You're the second group of them today. How can I help you?"

"I'm Luke Robertson, a police officer, and this is Jake Rogers, a private investigator," Luke explained. "I'll level with you, Pat. I'm off-duty, but my fiancée was the woman who died last night at Le Bijou Bistro. We're trying to find out who was responsible."

Pat exhaled. "Look, guys. I already told the police who were here earlier everything I know. They were swarming everywhere this morning, trying to close me down so they could search the place. I had to call my lawyer, who came down and told them to get out and not to come back without a search warrant. Unless you've got one, I suggest you leave."

"We just want to ask you a few questions," Jake said. "I realize you don't have to help us, Pat, but Luke has a personal stake in this. He just got engaged last night, right before his fiancée was murdered."

Pat's gaze shifted from Jake to Luke, and he relented. "Fine, but make it quick. We're already way behind today because of the police who came here earlier. What do you want to know?"

"Who ordered the cake that went to Le Bijou Bistro yesterday?" Jake asked, taking a spiral notebook and a ballpoint pen from his jacket pocket.

"Ah, that's the sixty-four-thousand-dollar question," Pat said. "I don't know where that cake came from, but it wasn't from here. I've checked the order book and the computer going way back. The last delivery we made to Le Bijou Bistro was over a week ago. The police have spoken to all the delivery drivers and verified that from their rosters. We don't even make chocolate cakes like the one in the picture the cops showed me. Ours are much fancier. I honestly think someone's trying to set me up."

Jake tapped the pen on his notebook, writing down what Pat had just said.

"Who do you think would want to do that?" Luke asked Pat.

Pat shrugged. "Might not be anyone I even know. Creative Cakes is one of the most popular specialty cake companies in the Seattle area. Looks like some crazy person made a cake with poison in it and sent it to a restaurant saying it's from here. Let's say, just for a minute, that we made that cake."

Jake's eyes narrowed as Pat continued.

"I'm hardly going to implicate my own business saying it was from here, am I?" Pat said.

"Good point," Jake said. "No one's saying you were aware of it, but could one of your staff have made it without your knowledge? Can you think of anyone who has a grudge against you and would like to see you in trouble?"

"Sure," Pat said, with a rueful smile, "but she doesn't work here." He rubbed his chin. "No, I don't think even Jessica would stoop that low."

"Who's Jessica?" Luke asked Pat.

Jake looked up from where he had been doodling the initials JS on his notepad. "Do you mean Jessica Simmons, your ex-wife?"

Pat sighed. "Even though we split up a long time ago, the woman still hates me. She divorced me for alleged unreasonable behavior, but I'm still not sure what I'm supposed to have done. She took our daughter away and turned her against me. Recently, Jessica seems to have gotten worse."

"What do you mean?" Jake asked. "Do you still see her?"

"Not if I can help it," Pat said. "However, she has a key for this place, so she can use the kitchen to test recipes for her blog. She only does it after our regular hours, so I'm rarely here at the same time she is."

"That's very generous of you," Luke commented.

"I've found, when it comes to Jessica, it's just easier to let her have her way. And she's still my daughter's mother. I had no idea she wanted to get back together until recently. It was all very embarrassing." Pat visibly reddened, and he shifted his weight from foot to foot.

Jake raised his eyebrows. "Can you tell us what happened?"

"Um, well she called me one evening sounding panicked. She said there'd been a small fire in the kitchen, and of course I came rushing down. When I arrived, there was no fire but she was, how shall I put it…waiting for me in a state of undress, in a provocative position in the frosting room."

"Okay, I think we get the picture," Jake said, trying to shake the same picture from his mind. "I take it you weren't tempted?"

"Not even close," Pat said. "I wrapped a blanket around her and explained as gently as possible that our relationship now is strictly platonic. She insisted I'd been coming on to her. The thing is, Jessica has some serious issues. She's delusional, to put it mildly. I really don't want to cause her any further distress."

Jake finished writing in his notebook, and flipped it shut. "Pat, this is very helpful, thank you. Do you mind if we get back to you if there's anything else?"

"That's fine," Pat said, deep in thought.

Jake remembered something else. "Oh, and my girlfriend has a big birthday coming up in a few weeks. Can I take a cake catalog with me?"

Pat nodded, and Jake tucked one under his arm.

Luke waited till they were outside before saying anything. "He seemed like a nice guy, and got kind of sad when he was talking about his ex-wife. Do you think she made the cake?"

"I have no idea," Jake said, striding toward the car. "But I fully intend to find out."

CHAPTER TWELVE

"Don't look at me with those sad eyes," DeeDee said. "I've already told you that you can't come with me today. I'm going to Seattle with Cassie."

Jake looked up from where he was reading the morning paper on the sofa in the great room. "Are you talking to me or to Balto?"

"Huh," DeeDee said as she sorted through some papers she'd laid out on the coffee table. "I might as well be talking to both of you. You're equally as bad when it comes to playing the sad eyes game with me. Balto and I have already been to the beach this morning, so he shouldn't be acting sad, but can you take him out again later? I promised I'd meet up with Roz, as well as seeing a Deelish client about a May barbecue. I can't seem to find the menu samples I prepared for them."

"How's Roz coping with being pregnant?" Jake inquired.

"She's doing really well. I can't wait to see her. She's tired from being in the early stages of her pregnancy, plus she's right in the middle of tax season, but that will end pretty soon. I think Clark wants her to quit working after the baby comes, but she won't hear of it. I wish I had that option."

"Well, I know you're not with me for my money, that's for sure,"

Jake said. "Because I don't have any."

DeeDee tossed some papers on the floor before picking up a glossy magazine and looking at the cover. "I knew it," she said excitedly, flipping through the pages.

"I don't think you'll find the menu you're looking for in Vogue," Jake commented, before going back to the crossword puzzle he was working on. "Hmm, nine across. Framework that supports a bridge, five letters. Got any idea what that would be?"

"Truss," DeeDee said, waving the magazine in Jake's face. "Here, look…I knew I'd seen it somewhere before!"

Jake adjusted his reading glasses and moved his head back. "Be careful with that thing, woman, or you're going to hit me in the eye. Why are you showing me an article about Elizabeth Taylor's jewelry collection?"

"Because…" DeeDee's tone was triumphant. She pointed to a picture of a huge diamond ring. "This is Cassie's ring. It went to sealed-bid auction recently along with several other pieces. Al must have bought it for her. Isn't that romantic?"

Jake frowned. "Let's hope he bought it, and didn't acquire it some other way. You know what Al's like." He raised his arm to shield himself from DeeDee's blows with the rolled-up magazine. "Ow. Just kidding. Ouch."

Balto came over to join in the fun. He leaped up, trying to catch the magazine in his mouth, thinking it was some sort of game.

"You have far too much energy, Balto," Jake said, managing to wrestle DeeDee's paper weapon from her grasp, while Balto landed on his lap. "How about you, me, and Red heading out for a while?" Balto jumped off of him and bounded into the hallway, wagging his tail.

DeeDee smiled, placing a handful of menu cards in the tote bag she used for work. "Found them. Are you going to be meeting with Luke again today?"

Jake raised his wrist and glanced at his watch. "Yes. We're going to visit Jules Moreau, and I need Rob to get more information on Jessica Simmons." Balto's head appeared around the doorway. "That's after I've taken Balto and Red out, of course," Jake said, grinning.

DeeDee turned at the sound of a car pulling up outside. "That'll be Cassie." A car door slammed, and DeeDee looked out the window. It was another clear day, and a beam of sunlight in the distance was reflecting off the sparkling blue water of Puget Sound.

A black town car with tinted windows was parked in front of the house. Cassie was walking up the steps of the porch, followed by a small wiry-looking man with a shiny bald head, who was carrying a sports bag. Jake joined her at the window, and DeeDee looked across at him, stifling a laugh.

"Do you think that's Harry the Hatchet? He looks more like a librarian."

"Maybe it's his cover," Jake said. "Although I agree…ugh, that mustard sweater." Jake made a face.

"Do you think his hatchet's in the bag?" DeeDee whispered. "It's so heavy it's almost trailing on the ground."

"Don't know. Maybe a submachine gun's in it."

DeeDee's mouth fell open as the sound of the doorbell rang through the house, and she watched Jake walk over to let them in, his shoulders shaking with laughter.

Cassie entered the house, smiling. "Hi, you two, this is Harry, a friend of Al's," she said. "He's our babysitter for the day."

DeeDee approached him to shake his hand, and saw Cassie give her a warning look. Harry took a step back, still gripping the bag.

"He's a man of few words, aren't you Harry?" Cassie said as she looked at Harry, who silently nodded.

"I've got to get going," Jake said, pulling on his coat. "Nice to meet you, Harry. Don't let these ladies give you any trouble."

Harry gave Jake a cold stare. Balto, who had followed the guests into the great room, sniffed Harry's feet before retreating to stand beside Jake.

"Bye, Cassie. Call you later, sweetheart," Jake said to DeeDee, kissing her on the cheek.

"You didn't have to come out all this way," DeeDee said when Jake had left. "I could have met you in Seattle. Do we have time for a coffee?"

Cassie shook her head. "Better not. I had to come out here to check on a few things on the house we're buying, anyway. I need your help with something, if you don't mind."

"Sure."

Cassie nodded to Harry, who set the bag down with a thud. He stooped down to unzip it, and DeeDee held her breath while he pulled out a couple of dark, heavy lumps.

"Which do you think, the antique pavers or the cobblestone?" Cassie said. "DeeDee, are you all right? These are for the patio," she explained. "I can't make up my mind."

DeeDee giggled, thinking about the conversation she and Jake had just had regarding what was in Harry's bag. "Definitely go with the antique pavers. I'll get my coat."

*****

"Ms. Ekenbach will see you now."

"Thanks, Darlene," Cassie said to the receptionist. "Ready?" she asked DeeDee.

"Yes," DeeDee said, following Cassie down the corridor. DeeDee glanced back at Harry, who remained seated in the reception area, his head motionless, but his eyes were constantly darting around the room. There was a black bag at his feet. It wasn't the sports bag he'd been carrying earlier. This one was smaller, but just as heavy. DeeDee had a feeling it didn't contain household items.

When they entered Gloria's office, a messy-haired blond stood up from her desk and greeted them warmly. She kissed Cassie on both cheeks, and gave DeeDee a strong handshake. It was so strong it caused DeeDee's arm to strain in its socket.

"Sit, sit, sit," Gloria said, motioning towards some chairs and a round table in the corner of the office. "Cassie, how are you holding up? That was such a horrible thing to have happen at a restaurant you were going to review. I completely understand that you won't be able to file a review on that one. I'm sure you agree that it would be terribly inappropriate."

Cassie nodded. "Yes, I—"

Gloria went on speaking, oblivious of Cassie's attempt to reply. "And this must be your friend, the wonderful DeeDee Wilson from Deelish. DeeDee, several of my friends have been raving about your catering. You'll have to give me one of your business cards."

DeeDee pulled one out from her purse. "Sure, here yo—"

Gloria had already turned her head back to Cassie. DeeDee put the card on the table and pushed it towards Gloria, before looking around the room. The immaculately decorated office was at odds with Gloria's unkempt personal appearance. It was the office

DeeDee would have dreamed of, if she had a dedicated space for her work at home. A giant iMac computer screen took center stage on a shiny white desk, the wireless keyboard and mouse tiny by comparison. A copper wire basket held some papers, and several pens poked out of the top of a papier-mâché pen holder, painted with gaudy childlike brushstrokes. A giant Stendig designer wall calendar adorned the wall behind the desk. Thick-pile ivory carpet and the white tulip table they were seated around, on cracked tan leather chairs, gave the place the feel of a magazine shoot. Given that Gloria was the newspaper's Lifestyle Editor, DeeDee supposed that wasn't far from the truth. She made a mental note to give her Deelish working area, aka the kitchen table, a more streamlined look.

"The thing is," Gloria was saying as DeeDee tuned back into the one-way conversation, "I'm so glad you came in. I've got a proposition for you, Cassie. How would you feel about taking on more work? Of course we'll make it worth your while."

Cassie opened her mouth to speak, but Gloria had merely paused for breath. She lowered her voice a little as she continued. "We're making some changes here, and the readers just love your column. Did you know that the cute waiter you mentioned a few weeks ago has his own Facebook fan page now with thousands of followers? You're what's known in the trade as an influencer, Cassie, and that's exactly what we need more of." Gloria smiled, revealing a smudge of lipstick on her front teeth. "What do you say?"

DeeDee and Cassie stared at Gloria, waiting for her to go on. Gloria clasped her hands together, and leaned in towards them. "Well?"

"I'm sorry, Gloria, but that won't be possible right now," Cassie said. "That's what I came here to tell you. After the incident at Le Bijou Bistro, my husband's worried for my safety."

Gloria, if you knew what was in Harry the Hatchet's bag in the reception area right now, you'd realize just how worried he is, DeeDee thought to herself, observing the editor, whose face had fallen.

"We agreed when I started working here that it was just a temporary thing, anyway," Cassie continued. "I'm not really looking for a full-time position. When is Myles Lambert planning on coming back?"

"He's not, that's just it," Gloria said thoughtfully. "I'm sure there must be a solution to this little problem. We really don't want to lose you, Cassie."

"What happened to Myles?" DeeDee asked. If Gloria told them he'd left and moved out of the state, maybe they had Megan's killer in their sights.

"It's kind of surprising," Gloria said. "He came to see me Monday morning. We had words last week, you see. I'd suggested he take longer to finish his foodie book, or whatever it was supposed to be. Truth is, I've been trying to discourage his return. I guess he sensed that too, and I could tell he wasn't very happy about it."

Cassie piped up. "Was he threatening to cause any sort of trouble?"

Gloria rubbed her teeth with her finger, removing the traces of lipstick. "No, not at all. Actually, he was very happy and excited. He pulled out a large box with a manuscript in it, and told me he'd been working on it all weekend. He said it was better than he remembered, and asked me to have a look at it for him. It was a murder mystery novel he's been trying to finish for years, and he thought he'd finally nailed it."

Cassie and DeeDee looked at each other, and DeeDee could see Cassie shift uncomfortably in her seat.

"Um, what was it about?" DeeDee asked.

"I don't want to give away any spoilers, but it was terribly clever," Gloria said. "A woman gets murdered in a restaurant. I was up all night reading it, because I could hardly put it down. I called an agent friend of mine, and by Wednesday morning there was a bidding war going on between three of the big traditional publishing houses. Hollywood's already called him about the movie rights for it. Seven figures."

"I see," DeeDee said, unable to believe what she was hearing. "That's...amazing."

"It sure is. Myles is laughing all the way to the bank." Gloria turned to Cassie. "In fact, he asked me to thank you for everything. He said if it wasn't for you, he probably never would have finished it. Of course, he won't be coming back to the paper now. This deal has him set up for life. He's living the writer's dream."

Cassie exhaled. "Good for him, that's marvelous. I was worried he might have a grudge against me or something."

Gloria leaned across the desk to pat Cassie's arm, causing the table to shake. "Oh no, quite the opposite. So you see, if you would rethink my offer, it would be a great outcome for everyone."

"I can't promise anything, but I'll discuss it with my husband," Cassie said. She looked down, distracted by the sound of her cell phone buzzing in her purse. "Sorry, do you mind if I get this?"

"Go ahead," Gloria said, picking up DeeDee's business card from the table and squinting at it.

"Briana, is that you, darling?" the excitement was audible in Cassie's voice, and DeeDee turned to her friend with a smile. In a matter of seconds, she watched the color drain from Cassie's face. The hand Cassie was using to hold her phone began to tremble. "Briana, please, calm down. Tell me where you are. It will be all right, I promise." She shook the cell phone in the air, and started frantically pressing some buttons, finally meeting DeeDee's worried gaze with a look of despair. "The line went dead," Cassie gasped, jumping up. "We have to go. Briana's in trouble."

CHAPTER THIRTEEN

"Mr. De Duco, it's been a while. Good to see you, sir. Your usual table on the patio?"

"Thanks, Doug." Al followed the General Manager of Ray's Café to the outdoor deck. A sailboat with a bright yellow sail bobbed past, its passengers a young couple wearing sweaters and shorts. Their laughter carried to where Doug was seating Al.

"Will anyone be joining you today, sir?" Doug asked, handing him a menu.

Al grunted. "Yeah, 'fraid so. Ima gonna' have a beer, and today's newspaper if ya' got it, please. Might be waitin' fer a bit."

Doug nodded, and placed a second menu on the table. "Coming right up, sir."

Al's beer and newspaper arrived within moments, and he sat in leisurely silence, looking up from the sports pages every now and then to take in the view of Puget Sound and the snow-capped Olympic mountain range beyond. Regular water traffic from the Ballard Locks sailed across his line of vision, as he tapped a reminder note into his phone.

Buy boat for Cassie. Small un'.

He hadn't been expecting Kitten Knight to be on time for their 11:30 a.m. meeting, but over an hour had passed, and the nearby tables had started to fill up when he heard the sound of her voice as she approached his table. Engaged in friendly conversation with Doug, the sound of Kitten's soft lilt was mesmerizing. Fixing his gaze firmly on the horizon, Al willed himself not to turn around. This was going to be harder than he'd expected.

"Like what you see?"

"Yep," Al said, without turning his head.

Kitten appeared opposite him, and wriggled into a chair, her revealing skin-tight top and jeans limiting her movement. "I wasn't talking about that view, Al. I'm talking about this view," she said, as she arched her back and pushed out her chest.

Al felt his heartbeat quicken. Kitten had made a special effort with her appearance, as he knew she would. Her platinum hair was in a casual updo that was just a little undone. Carefully applied no-makeup makeup made her skin look flawless, except for the smudged eyeliner and bee-stung lips. If Kitten was going for the just-got-out-of-bed look, she'd achieved it with a perfect ten.

"Ya' look like a million bucks, tax-free," he said, before turning to Doug. "A blanket fer the lady, please. She forgot to finish gettin' dressed."

Kitten raised an eyebrow. "You never had any complaints about that before."

Al took a swig of his beer. "That was different."

"What's that supposed to mean?"

Al looked at Kitten, and felt a pang of...he wasn't sure what. Before he met Cassie, Kitten was one of his favorite people. For years, off and on, they'd enjoyed one another's company, both inside and outside the bedroom. Fun to be with, Kitten was a witty and intelligent conversationalist who was always up on current events, as well as being easy on the eye and providing a warm body to cuddle up to after dark. But she wasn't Cassie.

"Cat got your tongue, Al? It's not like you to be so shy." Kitten turned her megawatt smile toward the waiter who was approaching the table. He was holding a glass of white wine on a tray. "Thank you," she said to the server, in a voice as sweet as honey, before sultrily sipping her drink, as she maintained eye contact with the waiter. The young man's face flushed as he stumbled away.

Remorse. Al realized he hadn't handled the Kitten situation well.

"Kitty, Ima sorry. I shoulda' tol' ya' straight 'bout me an' Cassie. I never meant to hurt ya'."

"Bit late for that, I think." Kitten's tone became hard. She scrolled through the screen on her phone on the table. "How many times did I try to call you, Al, to get closure? And what did I get? I'll tell you what I got, one crummy voice message with instructions never to contact you again. What did you expect, that I'd just crawl away without a fight? I warned you that no good would come of how you treated me."

Al's thoughts of remorse disappeared. The cold look in Kitten's eyes was enough to make him remember why they were there. "Yeah, ya' did. Never had ya' as a killer, though. Who did ya' get to do it?" He removed his sunglasses, and stared Kitten down, eyeball to eyeball.

Kitten looked away first. "I don't know what you mean," she mumbled, waving to the waiter. "Are we going to eat, or are you sticking to humble pie?"

Al smiled, despite himself. "I always admired yer' spirit, Kitty."

Kitten's face softened. "The usual?"

Al nodded.

Even though Kitten had a strict policy of sleeping late and only eating one meal a day, dinner, she had been known to break the habit if an attractive man was involved.

"Two cups of Ray's Clam Chowder and a Classic Caesar to share," Kitten said to the waiter, handing him back the menus. "Thank you." She turned to Al. "What was that you were saying about murder?"

"I never mentioned murder, you did."

Kitten shrugged. "If you thought I might have considered killing you or your new wife, you'd be right."

"So did ya' act on it, or not?"
Kitten wrapped the blanket Doug had brought out around her shoulders. "Believe me, I thought plenty about it."

"Quit dodgin' the question, Kitten. Someone put a hit on my wife two nights ago, and it seems like they mighta' been after me too. Somethin' tells me that person coulda' been you."

Kitten tapped her lip with her finger. "You mean the unfortunate death that occurred at Le Bijou Bistro? You know I'd never be so dumb as to get my hands dirty like that," she said, reaching for a bread roll. "I was busy Wednesday night, as it happens. I trust you know that you weren't the only man in my life."

"I do," Al said. "And that's why I'm surprised yer' takin' this all so personal. I thought me an' you had an understandin'. No strings. Went both ways."

"Maybe I wanted more, Al. Except I never knew it was an option."

Al let out an exasperated sigh. "Neither did I. Kitty, I'm tellin' ya', it just happened. Minute I met Cassie was the first I'd thought about settlin' down, ever."

Kitten jutted her chin out. "You sure know how to make a

woman feel special."

"I didn't mean it like that, Kitty. Somethin' just clicked. Cassie makes me complete, that's jes' how it is. I'm sorry if I've hurt ya', but I'm not sorry 'bout bein' with Cassie." He waited while the waiter placed their soups and salad on the table before continuing. "Here's how it is. Anyone messes with my wife, they got me to answer to." He lifted his knife, and pointed it at Kitten.

"Don't I know it," Kitten said, tasting her soup. "Delicious." She smiled. "What's done is done. I should thank you, Al, for helping me see the error in my ways. From now on, I'm a one-man woman. And that man most certainly isn't you."

Al chuckled. "Kitty, Ima glad yer' heart healed so quick. Who's the lucky feller?"

"It's not official," Kitten said, tilting her head to one side. "But I've been thinking it over the past few days. There's plenty of worse places to live than Waterfront Palace, don't you think? I've met with the designer, and she's sent me some fabulous design boards for the interior, so I thought to myself, why spoil a good thing?"

"With somethin' nasty like murder, you mean?"

"Exactly," Kitten nodded. "We had some good times, didn't we?" She caught Al's eye, and he reached for his sunglasses, putting them back on.

"Sure we did," he muttered. The conversation was in danger of going places he didn't want to revisit. The past was in the past, where it belonged.

Kitten glanced at his ring finger. "If it weren't for that," she said pointedly, "we could almost forget you were married, and who knows where the rest of the day might lead."

Al choked on his soup. "Keep talkin' like that and Ima leavin'." Gazing at Kitten, a thought occurred to him. "The Waterfront Palace is one of Mario Carlucci's developments, am I right?"

Kitten, picked at a salad leaf, pretending not to hear.

"Kitty, ya' sure know how to hit a man where it hurts." Al couldn't help the blow to his pride resulting from Kitten's revelation. The fact she'd obviously joined Team Mario rankled him, even if Al didn't want her for himself. Judging from the upward turn at the sides of Kitten's mouth, his comment pleased her. "Is that who you were with Wednesday night?"

"Al, jealousy doesn't suit you. Like I said, nothing's been finalized. I haven't seen Mario for a little while, but that's irrelevant. We have the rest of our lives together, so no hurry. Feels good, doesn't it?"

"It does." Al raised his beer glass to Kitten. "Here's to happy futures. For both of us, jes' not together."

Kitten clicked her glass against his. "Happy futures. I guess we can't be friends?"

"That'd be a stretch." Al set down his glass, relaxing back in the chair.

"What's she like, your wife?" Kitten asked, pushing away her soup cup and dabbing her lips with a napkin.

"Cassie? Smart, beautiful, and funny, for starters. Softer, yet stronger than anyone I ever met. I'd go on, but then you really would want to kill her."

"It's okay," Kitten said softly. "I'm glad. Happy looks good on you, Al."

"Thanks," Al said, enjoying the warmth of the afternoon sun. "Will ya' have another glass of wine?"

Kitten shrugged the blanket off her shoulders and shook her head, standing up. She held his gaze just long enough for her face to crumple. "No, I'd better go. Be seeing you, Al."

"So long, Kitty."

It was Al who turned as Kitten walked away, and Kitten who didn't look back. Al finished his beer in quiet contemplation, and noticed that the pang he'd felt earlier in his chest was gone. Glancing down at the sound of the ringtone of his cell phone, he picked it up when Cassie's name flashed across the screen.

"Yo," he answered with a lazy smile, as he debated whether or not to order another beer. He leaned back as Cassie's voice came on the line. Her high-pitched delivery of the news about Briana sent shivers up his back. "Ima comin' right now," he shouted, scrambling to his feet, and throwing a handful of cash on the table.

He ran into the parking lot, where Kitten was just leaving in a sleek Mercedes sports car. Jumping into his Maserati and switching on the ignition, he floored the accelerator and sped away, tires screeching.

CHAPTER FOURTEEN

"Tell me about Megan," Jake said to Luke, who was driving. "Were you two together long?"

They were on their way to Frogities to talk to Jules Moreau. The Luke who had met Jake at the same place at the Seattle Waterfront Marriott the previous day was unshaven and looked as if he hadn't slept. Jake hoped that talking about Megan would keep the younger man calm, since Luke's erratic driving suggested his temper was frayed. He'd already flashed his police badge twice in order to get through the downtown traffic, and was muttering comments about other drivers under his breath. The last thing Jake wanted was for Luke to get involved in some type of incident that would increase his current problems.

The mention of Megan caused Luke to loosen his grip on the steering wheel enough for his arm to relax instead of being rigid. Jake smiled at him encouragingly.

"We met at my sister's birthday party almost three years ago. Megan and my sister, Hannah, went to nursing school together. There were a lot of pretty women there that night, but I couldn't take my eyes off Megan. Her smile lit up the room."

"Did Megan work in Seattle?" Jake asked.

"Yep. Seattle Children's Hospital, in the ICU Department. The stories Megan came home with would break your heart. It was hard for her to get work out of her head at the end of the day. In some cases, the hospital was the only home those children ever knew."

"That's a tough job," Jake said. "It takes a special kind of person to do it."

"That's right." Luke roughly wiped his cheek with the back of his hand. "Jake, would you mind driving? I'm having trouble concentrating."

"Of course."

Luke pulled the car over to the side of the street and got out, and Jake moved over to the driver's seat. As soon as Luke had fastened his seat belt, he leaned his head back and closed his eyes. "Thanks, Jake. Tell me when we get to Bellevue."

Jake pulled the Honda into the flow of traffic, got on the freeway and within a short while they were in Bellevue. Jake drove past the quirky brick restaurant front that was Frogties and found a parking space a little further down the street beside a row of stores. He glanced over at Luke and realized he was sound asleep. He decided Luke could do with a little more shut-eye time, so he quietly got out of the car and stretched his legs.

Several trucks had pulled up in front of Frogties. Jake assumed the daily deliveries were still being made, so he walked in the opposite direction, towards a coffee shop on the corner. He ordered a cup of coffee and sat down at the counter by the window. He took a sip as he pulled out his phone and made a call.

"Hi, Rob. Were you able to come up with anything else on Jessica Simmons?"

"Just a moment, Jake, I'm on another call."

Jake sipped his coffee as he waited for Rob. A woman pushing a toddler in a stroller walked by with an older child riding on the back of it on a stand-on platform. All three of them were singing the Itsy-Bitsy Spider song, with an out-of-tune gusto.

Rob came back on the line. "Sorry about that. Our friend Jessica Simmons seems to have gone offline. Her blog is still there, but she hasn't posted anything since the beginning of the week. I've been looking back at some of her posts, and there's one ominous recipe that's jumping out at me."

"What's that?"

"Killer Chocolate Cake," Rob said, pausing for effect. "She uploaded the recipe about a week ago along with a video of her making the cake. She said it's a Simmons family favorite, and no one has ever died from it yet."

"I'm assuming that was a joke, right?"

"Maybe Jessica's, but not mine. She really said it."

"Good work," Jake said. "I think it's about time I paid Jessica a visit. I need you to call the Police Department and give them that cake recipe, see if the ingredients match the cake that killed Jessica. Apart from the cyanide, of course."

"I thought cake was just eggs, butter, flour, and sugar. Jessica's cake had all those things, with added chocolate. Not exactly incriminating, Jake, if you know what I mean."

Jake rubbed his chin. "True, but there's no harm running it past them anyway. Luke and I are at Moreau's restaurant now. We'll head over to Jessica's after we finish here. Would you send me her address?"

"Sure. Let me know if you need anything else."

"Thanks, Rob. Keep checking on Jessica." Jake got a refill for his coffee and bought another one to take out to the car for Luke. He tapped gently on the car window, and grinned when Luke jumped. Like any police officer, Luke's instinct was to reach for his gun when he was startled, and his hand instinctively had reached inside his leather jacket. When he saw Jake, he smiled, and his gesture changed into a stretch.

"Let's go," Jake said, when Luke got out of the car and he'd handed him the coffee. "I'm not sure what's going on at Frogities, but there sure seems to be a lot of people milling around."

They walked down the street to where two white trucks were still parked in front of it. The back door of one of the trucks was open, revealing several large pieces of recording equipment. Jake pushed through a group of people which included a cameraman and a woman with a long furry boom microphone, motioning to Luke to follow him. Luke had a puzzled expression on his face. Once they were inside the restaurant, they both raised their hands to shield their eyes. The glaring studio lights were blinding.

"Do you think we've made a mistake and walked onto a television set instead of a restaurant?" a confused Jake asked Luke, who shrugged, and tapped a nearby woman on the shoulder.

"Ssh," she hissed at him, turning around. "Can't you see we're filming?"

"Police," Luke said, flashing his badge in her face. "Can you tell us where we can find Mr. Moreau, please?"

"Are you in this scene?" The woman looked them over and smiled. "Because if you're not, two hot guys like you should be. Makeup is over there, at the counter. Tell them you're extras, and that Victoria sent you."

"I'm not an actor," Luke said, putting his badge back in his pocket. "I really am a police officer."

The woman's mouth fell open. "Oh, I'm sorry." Her face turned crimson. "Mr. Moreau is in the kitchen."

"Thanks," Luke said, nodding. Jake followed him through the small restaurant, past the bar area, through double doors at the back, and into the kitchen. They were met with more lights and cameras, and the sound of a Frenchman hurling insults at the chef.

"You cannot be serious," he screamed. "This sauce is disgusting. Deeees-gust-eeeng. If you want to keep your Michelin star, as well as your job, you need to make it again. Do you understand?"

The chef, dressed in starched whites and wearing a towering white hat, lifted a boiling pan from the stove and poured its contents down the sink. "You don't like it?" the chef taunted Moreau. "Then why don't you make it?"

The chef tore off his hat and threw it on the floor, stomping past Moreau with a glare.

"CUT!" called a man in jeans holding a clipboard. There was some cheering, and Moreau approached the chef and gave him a huge grin and a high-five. "Great, guys, that's a wrap," said the clipboard man. "We'll take five."

Jake approached the man with the French accent, who was wearing a very expensive looking suit. "Mr. Moreau?"

Jules Moreau turned and nodded. "That's me." He glanced from Jake to Luke, who was holding his police badge, and his eyes narrowed.

"If we could have a few moments of your time, sir," Luke said.

"Follow me," Jules said in a clipped tone, heading for the double doors. When they were back inside the restaurant, he led Jake and Luke to a table away from the lights. "How can I help you, gentlemen?" he asked, when they were seated. "As you heard, I only have five minutes, so please make it quick."

Luke took the lead. "Mr. Moreau, we're investigating the murder of a woman at Le Bijou Bistro two nights ago. I assume you're aware of what happened?"

Moreau shrugged. "I might have heard something, but I haven't given it much attention. I've been too busy filming my new television show all week. It's going to be called Jules' Kitchen."

"Well I've been giving it a lot of attention, Mr. Moreau, since the murder victim was my fiancée," Luke said calmly.

Jules' face softened, and his eyes dropped. "I'm sorry," he murmured.

Jake spoke up. "Mr. Moreau, it's come to our attention there's been an ongoing feud between you and another restaurateur, Bertrand Christolhomme, the owner of Le Bijou Bistro. Is that correct?"

Jules thought for a moment, and looked up at Jake. "I wouldn't call it a feud, but more like a healthy rivalry. Passions run high in French culture."

"High enough for you to exact revenge on your rival by arranging for an incident to occur in his restaurant that would cause his business to fail?" Jake asked.

Jules replied without hesitation. "I admit there may have been a time when a thought like that crossed my mind, but sometimes things happen for a reason."

"Would you like to explain that, Mr. Moreau?" Luke leaned in. "If you know of some reason why my fiancée should be murdered, I'd love to hear about it."

"You misunderstood me," Jules said in an apologetic tone of voice. "I simply meant the result of my ongoing differences with Bertrand was that a reality television company contacted me after the Restaurant Awards event took place last week. They offered me a pilot show, which is what we're in the middle of filming at the moment. If it's a success, there's a possibility the show could be extended to a full season. I think it's obvious I don't need to sabotage Le Bijou Bistro to achieve my goals. This opportunity is bigger than I ever could have dreamed of."

Jake glanced at Luke, who nodded. They'd heard enough. Moreau wasn't their man. He was too interested in being the next star of reality television to have been involved in Megan's death.

"We won't take up any more of your time, Mr. Moreau," Luke said, standing up. "Thanks for talking to us. We'll see ourselves out."

They made their way through the cameras and lights in silence.

"What's next?" Luke asked, as they walked out into the street. Jake blinked his eyes several times to adjust to the daylight.

"I think it's time to visit Jessica Simmons," Jake said, pulling his phone out of his pocket. "Let me just take this incoming call."

He listened to DeeDee in silence, his face turning grim. "Keep me posted," he said, striding in the direction of the car.

"Jake, is everything all right?" Luke asked, struggling to keep up with him.

Jake shook his head. "My friend's daughter has been kidnapped. If we don't find her soon, we could be looking at another homicide."

Luke stopped and grabbed Jake's arm. "I think it's time you told me more about these friends of yours, and exactly what's going on."

Jake pressed the key fob he was holding in his hand, opening the doors of Luke' car. "I think you're right. Get in, and I'll tell you everything on the way to Jessica's."

CHAPTER FIFTEEN

Briana Roberts felt around in the darkness of the room where she'd woken up earlier, trying to get a sense of where she was and how she'd gotten there. Her hands were tied behind her back, making everything more difficult. Right now all she wanted was some water and to get rid of the nylon cord that was binding and chafing her wrists. She'd wrestled with it trying to get it off, but all she'd managed to do was pull the knot even tighter.

From what she could tell, she was in a basement or storage room of some kind. The only light came from a small window near the ceiling, which was open an inch or two. Even if she could climb up there, it was too small for anything bigger than a cat to squeeze through, plus she wouldn't have the use of her hands. She walked around in the semi-darkness bumping into taped-up boxes, and other household items. She'd already tripped over a bucket and the mop that was next to it.

The damp air and musty smell of mold was causing her to have trouble catching her breath. Although she hadn't had an incident in years, she was terrified her childhood asthma might be threatening to make a reappearance. She had no inhaler, and she could feel her panic beginning to rise. Briana edged her way along one of the walls in the room, past the locked door she'd banged her feet against for what seemed like hours, and then found her way back to the chair she'd been sitting on when she came to, her head throbbing. She remembered having been hit on the back of her head, but by whom, or by what, she had no idea.

Crouching down and feeling for the seat of the chair, she eased herself down slowly to avoid landing on her behind on the cold concrete floor. If she knocked the chair over, there was no way for her to pick it back up again. Tears of tiredness, frustration, and pain rolled down her cheeks when she finally was able to sit down on the wobbly seat.

Stop feeling sorry for yourself, Briana, the voice in her head told her. *There's no time for tears. You're the only one who can help you, because no one knows where you are.*

Initially, she'd congratulated herself on her ingenuity for being able to make a call to her mom. First came the initial feat of fishing her cell phone out of the back pocket of her pants, which took quite a bit of dexterity and tenacity. Then she'd lain down on the floor, and as gently as she could, put the phone down so it didn't break. She'd been able to unlock the phone by using her thumbprint, but making a call was another matter, since she couldn't see the screen if she held it in her hands behind her back.

She'd kicked off one Nike shoe and wriggled off her sock, so she could press the screen with her big toe, holding the phone in place with her other foot. The light from the phone showed that there was barely any battery power left and minimal network reception. Numerous attempts to call her mother failed, until she finally got a signal just long enough to tell Cassie she'd been kidnapped before the line went dead.

Briana tried to figure out what day it was. She was fairly certain she'd only been wherever she was for one night. The day before, Thursday, was when she had started thinking something weird was happening, like perhaps she was being followed.

She'd had a meeting in the morning at the Waterfront Palace with Ms. Knight, a friend of the developer, Mario Carlucci. Briana remembered thinking how nice the woman was, and how pretty she was for her age.

"Just call me Kitty," Ms. Knight had told her when she arrived holding a cup of Starbucks coffee. The two of them had bonded over fabric swatches, quartz countertops, and light fixtures from the best stores in town. Kitty had ooh'd and ahh'd over Briana's selections, and loved Briana's idea of opening up the walk-in closet with an entrance to the second bath. Briana felt her life would be a lot easier if all her clients were like Kitty.

"Would you like me to order these?" Briana asked, when they were finished looking at the different samples. Kitty had great taste, and cost didn't seem to be an issue.

Kitty simply laughed. "I'd better give the good news to your boss first. Is Mr. Carlucci around?"

"He was on site earlier," Briana said, "but I think he went back to his office. Would you like me to let him know you were here? I didn't know that you two were friends, or I would have mentioned you were coming in when I saw him this morning."

"That's okay," Kitty said. "I just might surprise him later. Please, don't say a word." She gave Briana a conspiratory wink.

"Certainly," Briana said, smiling, as she put her samples away. There was obviously something going on between Ms. Knight and her boss, and she decided she was probably better off staying out of it.

When Briana went into the office to drop off the samples after the meeting, Mr. Carlucci wasn't there. She decided she'd worked long enough and it was time for her daily run. After she'd changed into her running clothes, she stuck her head through the sales manager's door and said, "I'm going out for a run, Sam. I don't have any appointments for the rest of the afternoon, but I'll probably check back in later."

Sam had barely looked up from his spreadsheets. "Sure, take your time," he said, waving her away. Thinking back on it, Briana wondered if the conversation had even registered with him.

She took her usual route along the waterfront, but something felt off. She looked around a few times, unable to shake the bad feeling she had. As far as she could see, the rest of the world was going about its business in a very normal fashion.

That was when she realized what was probably bugging her. She felt bad about having deliberately missed her mother's birthday the day before. Although she was still mad at Cassie for getting married so soon after her father's murder, the truth was she missed her. They'd always had a very close relationship. Briana had stopped to get a juice drink and called Cassie, but no one had answered. She'd laughed thinking that her mother probably had turned off her phone and forgotten to turn it back on.

The last thing Briana remembered was returning to her office by way of the basement parking garage entrance and hearing footsteps coming up fast from behind her. Her heart was pounding, and she realized she was in danger. She pressed redial on her phone to call her mom for help and again, there was no answer. She jammed her phone into the back pocket of her jogging shorts and ran for the elevator, but she could still hear the footsteps behind her, and they were rapidly gaining on her. She was afraid to turn around, so she never saw the object that hit her head before she fell to the floor, unconscious.

And now, here she was, goodness knows where, with no means of escape. To make matters worse, she had no water. She'd read that people couldn't live very long without water.

A sound from above broke into her thoughts. Her eyes flickered from side to side in the darkness. There it was again, the sound of a door being opened and shut. She heard someone walking around. Briana jumped up and started to kick her feet against the door, yelling at the top of her lungs.

"Help, please, help me. I'm down here." Her breathing was

erratic, and her voice was hoarse.

She stopped yelling and listened as the sound of footsteps got closer. The footsteps seemed to be coming from a stairway that led to where she was being held captive. She heard a key turning in the lock, and the door in front of her swung open.

For a moment there was silence, then Briana gasped when she saw the person standing in front of her. "What on earth are you doing here?" she blurted out.

CHAPTER SIXTEEN

When they were outside The Seattle Times building, and after she'd called Jake to tell him Briana had been kidnapped, DeeDee took control of the situation. "Cassie, do you have a key for Briana's apartment?"

Cassie nodded. "Yes, it's back at the hotel."

"I think we should get it," DeeDee said. "Maybe there's something at Briana's place that might give us a clue as to where she is. In the meantime, keep trying to call her. Harry, we need you to take us to Cassie's hotel right now."

Harry nodded, holding an arm out to shield Cassie from the throng of shoppers and office workers in the crowded street as they went to the car. They didn't have far to go to get to The Four Seasons, but the Friday traffic would have made the short trip a crawl if it wasn't for Harry's driving prowess. DeeDee marveled at how he squeezed the town car through spaces she would have thought were impossible, even for a much smaller car, like a Mini. She gripped the edge of the leather seat as the car raced through a red light, narrowly missing a little old lady who had just stepped into the crosswalk, and then screeched around a corner ricocheting off a parked car.

"Harry drives like Al," she said in a low voice to Cassie, who had Briana on constant redial, but with no success.

"They must have gone to the same getaway driver school," Cassie said with a faint smile.

When she looked up, DeeDee saw Harry's cold eyes looking back at hers in the rear view mirror. She quickly looked out the window, deciding to keep quiet until they reached their destination. Apparently, Harry didn't share Al's sense of humor.

Harry left the engine running when he pulled into the valet parking area at the hotel. He opened the door for Cassie, and the two of them hurried inside. "I'll wait here," DeeDee mumbled to no one, alone in the empty car. While they were gone, she called her client to postpone their afternoon appointment as well as her sister, Roz, to postpone their lunch date.

"Hey, sis," she said, when Roz picked up the call. "I'm really sorry, but something urgent has come up. Can I take a rain check on this afternoon?"

"Fine," Roz said with a pretend sigh. "You caught me just before I was leaving to meet you. I'll forgive you, but only on one condition."

"Name it," DeeDee said, seeing Cassie's figure appear in the revolving front door of the hotel.

"Lunch is on you next time." Roz giggled. "And I'm warning you, my appetite is huge. I'm eating for two, remember?"

DeeDee smiled. "I remember, and I can't wait to see you and the sonogram pictures." Cassie and Harry were racing toward the car. "Um, Roz, I really have to go now, sorry."

"Wait, DeeDee, what's going on? I know that tone of voice." Roz let out an exaggerated groan. "Not again. You're not mixed up in another murder, are you?"

Cassie jumped into the car and shut the door. She looked at DeeDee and raised her eyebrows.

"Bye, Roz, I'll call you as soon as I can. I promise." DeeDee ended the call despite the sound of Roz's loud protests, and turned back to Cassie. "Were you able to get it?"

"Yes." Some color had returned to Cassie's cheeks, which may have been the result of her recent run. Harry slammed his door, and once again the car raced off. "I spoke to Al. He's going to meet us at Briana's apartment," Cassie said, impatiently tapping her fingers on the seat.

Harry worked his magic once more, weaving through the traffic like a grand prix driver. At one point, when they came to a standstill, he gently rear-ended the vehicle in front of them, moving it far enough ahead to create a space that allowed their car to enter the bus lane, where it zoomed past the regular traffic.

"I think it's better if we don't talk about traffic violations right now," DeeDee murmured to Cassie, who she could see was in the process of leaning forward to tap Harry's shoulder in protest. "I know you're an advocate for civic duty and responsibility, but we need to get there as quickly as possible, right?"

Cassie, a regular animal rights campaigner, dog rescue center volunteer, and all-around do-gooder, paused for a moment. "Okay," she said, sitting back again. "I can't say I approve, but since it's definitely an emergency, I guess anything goes." She raised her voice again, so Harry could hear her. "You may as well step on it, Harry."

"Yes, ma'am," Harry said with a grin. Those were the first words DeeDee had heard him speak. He hit the gas, and DeeDee closed her eyes for the rest of the trip, which was accented with car horns blaring as Harry cut in front of other drivers. At one point, she hoped the nearby sirens she heard had nothing to do with them.

When the car finally came to a stop, DeeDee opened one eye, and saw Al pacing outside the apartment building. Cassie had already flung her door open and went running towards Al, who pulled her into a tight embrace. By the time DeeDee got out, Al and Cassie were headed inside, and DeeDee had to hurry to catch up.

They took the elevator to the second floor, where two doors opened onto a small, central hallway. "It's 2B," Cassie said, pointing to the second door. Al had it open within seconds, and they stepped inside a deceptively spacious apartment with a bright, airy living room, a kitchen area off to the side, and a hallway leading to what DeeDee assumed was the bedroom and bathroom. Briana's home was decorated in a Scandinavian style—white walls and pale blond wooden flooring, with a plush cream wool rug and contrasting blush colored throws and neutral pillows. The focal point of the living area, a giant abstract ocean painting, took DeeDee's breath away. The blues and grays covered the spectrum of angry to serene, and pulled her in. She looked at the name of the artist. It wasn't one she recognized, nor did she consider it an appropriate time to ask Cassie if she knew where Briana had acquired it.

"What are we looking for?" Cassie asked as she lifted a black hardbound appointment book from the small dining room table in the corner.

"Anythin' at all," Al said. "We'll know when we find it. Looks like whoever was tryin' to kill Cassie decided to go after Briana when their plan backfired. Poor Megan Reilly was murdered fer nothin'. We need to talk to Briana's friends and the people she worked with to figure out who saw her last, and when and where. Heck, I don't care if it's the local barista, Ima gonna' go through every name in that book and call every last contact we can think of til' we trace her." His eyes shone with sincerity and hope. "So don'tcha worry, Cassie, okay?"

Cassie nodded. "Here you go," she said, handing the appointment book to Al. "I'm going to start with her personal effects in the bedroom, and you and DeeDee can cover this room." She glanced around. "Those papers on the table look like they could be work-related."

DeeDee sat at the table, and started in on the pile of paperwork. There were invoices, letters from suppliers, bank statements, but nothing that struck her as out of the ordinary for a young self-employed woman in her twenties.

Al, who was on the sofa reading Briana's appointment book, suddenly sat bolt upright. "Cassie," he said in a loud voice, "where did you say Briana was working at the moment?"

Cassie appeared at the end of the hallway. "I didn't. She usually had a couple of design projects going on at the same time, but the last time I talked to her about her business, she mentioned she had a big one somewhere on the waterfront. To tell the truth, I didn't pay much attention to it. That was several weeks ago. She's been avoiding me, as you know."

"Ima gonna' kill him," Al growled, standing up and balling one hand into a fist. "That dirty, no-good, son-of-a-gun Carlucci. I shoulda' known he was capable of doin' somethin' like this, and now it's too late for me to kick his sorry behind outta shape. I coulda' finished him off years ago, but I always felt sorry for the dumb loser after he lost his girl."

"What are you talking about, Al? Who's Carlucci?" Cassie asked as she stepped up close to him.

"He owns a new high-end apartment development, called the Waterfront Palace," Al explained. "Accordin' to Briana's appointment book, it's her latest interior design project. He's also an old enemy of mine from years back. Blames me for his girlfriend gettin' killed. And more recently, he probably blames me for losin' his latest squeeze, Kitten Knight. I met her earlier today, and although she's decided to give her relationship with him another go, he's not aware of it yet."

DeeDee was getting more confused by the second. "What's this Knight woman got to do with you, Al?"

"She's an ex of Al's," Cassie said, "who's been bothering him ever since she found out we got married. She was one of the persons of interest in the death of Megan Reilly that Al was following up on."

"I'm pretty sure we can rule her out," Al said, "although accordin' to Briana's appointment book, she was due to meet Kitten yesterday mornin'. I can find out if that meetin' went ahead easily enough. If it did, she could be one of the last people to have seen Briana."

DeeDee felt a hard object underneath the pile of papers she was looking through. Moving some magazine clippings and unopened envelopes out of the way, she uncovered an iPad. Raising it in the air, she looked over to Cassie with a smile. "Look what I just found."

Cassie's face broke into a grin. "Are you thinking what I'm thinking?"

DeeDee nodded excitedly. "Yes." She started tapping. When she looked back up at Cassie and Al, her eyes were dancing. "We're in business. Briana has installed the Find My iPhone app on her iPad. This should give us an exact location of her phone."

Cassie and Al came over to the table beside DeeDee, who was activating the search function. Nothing happened.

"It's not working," DeeDee said, burying her head in her hands. "If Briana's device is out of battery power or without a network or Wi-Fi coverage, it won't connect."

"We can get her phone company to run a trace on the phone," Al said. "DeeDee, were there any phone records in that pile of paperwork?"

"Yes, I think so. Let me find them."

"Stop," Cassie said, her finger tapping the iPad tablet screen. "It's…it's connecting. There must an intermittent signal on Briana's end. That suggests she's somewhere remote. Quick, get the directions while I try and get her on the line again." Cassie thrust the device at DeeDee and she reached for her cell phone.

DeeDee's eyes widened. "We've got a location. Briana's on Orcas Island. I've got the GPS coordinates for the exact location on the island. I'll let Jake know. Shall we go?" She looked up only to discover that Al and Cassie were already heading for the door.

CHAPTER SEVENTEEN

Ashley Simmons picked the heavy laundry basket up off of the floor of Shell's Laundromat and tipped its contents into the industrial size washing machine. It was just after 10:00 a.m., and it was her fourth large wash load of the day. She slammed the door shut and put the machine on the hot water setting before moving onto the next basket, repeating the procedure all over again.

"That's a pretty big sigh for a Friday morning" Shelly, her boss, said as she looked up from the counter where she was counting a pile of coins that had been emptied out of the machines. "Cheer up, it's payday. Have any big plans for the weekend?"

Ashley's shoulders sagged, and she shook her head. "Nope. I was going to ask if you wanted me to work tomorrow. I could kind of use the money."

Shelly bagged the last of the coins and locked them in the safe under the counter, before coming out to help Ashley. "Is everything all right, Ash? I'm worried about you. You've been down lately, and I hate to see you looking so unhappy. Why don't you tell Auntie Shell all about it, huh?"

Ashley handed Shelly one end of a bed sheet and they started to fold it. Ashley felt Shelly's kind eyes on her, and she wished her mother cared for her even a fraction of what Shelly did. In the two years Ashley had worked at the laundromat, Shelly had been more of a mother figure to her than Jessica had been her entire life.

It was several long moments before Ashley spoke. "Jackson and I broke up last night," she said eventually.

They were interrupted by a customer who was having trouble operating one of the dryer machines. "I put my money in, but it's not working," said a hostile young man wearing a hooded jacket pulled up over his head.

Ashley, being used to dealing with challenging customers, smiled at him tightly. "Let me help you with that, sir," she said, going over to the machine and sizing up the situation. "I think you forgot to put the money in," she said in an even voice.

The youth turned towards Ashley. "You callin' me a liar?" he asked. He jutted his chin out and sneered at her.

"Of course not." She stared coldly back at him, and entered the code for the free setting on the machine. The drum started to spin around. "There you go, sir."

The youth smirked and walked outside where Ashley saw him light up a hand-rolled cigarette. She walked back over to Shelly, who had finished folding the basket of clean laundry and was waiting for Ashley to return.

"What happened with Jackson?" Shelly sat on the wooden bench, and patted the seat beside her. "Sit, Ash."

Ashley did as she was instructed. "I caught him stealing my money again," she mumbled, staring at the floor. "It disappears as quick as I earn it. I told him I'd had enough, and to get a job and pay me back, or to get out."

Shelly bent her head down and looked across at Ashley. "What did he say?"

Eyes turned downward, Ashley kicked the floor with her scuffed tennis shoe. "A lot of nasty stuff that I won't repeat. It was mostly the usual sort of insults he likes to throw around, about me being worthless, and that I'd be nothing without him."

"Hmm. I hope you set him straight about that"

Ashley looked up and met Shelly's eye, a shy smile crossing her face. "Yes, for once I did. I don't know what happened, but something in me snapped, and I let him have it with both barrels. I told him he had it all backwards. I told him he was holding me back, and I wanted more out of my life than to be stuck with a loser like him. I told him to leave and to never come back."

"How did that make you feel?" Shelly said.

Ashley shrugged. "It felt good at first. He thought I wasn't serious and that I'd calm down, but when I stuffed his things in a drawstring duffel bag and threw them out the door, he got the message. He started to sweet-talk me and begged me to reconsider. When I told him no, he turned nasty again. Now it's over, and I'm sad, lonely and a little bit scared."

Shelly brushed Ashley's hair out of her eyes. "Ash, you're what...twenty-two?"

Ashley nodded.

"You've got your whole life ahead of you. Don't let anyone drag you down, or tell you you're not good enough. Sleazy manipulators like Jackson prey on women with low self-esteem. They're bullies, and they take advantage of vulnerable people. I'm proud of you, Ash, for standing up to him like that. It's the first step in taking back control of your life. What did your mom say when you told her?"

"I haven't seen her since yesterday morning," Ashley said. "I stopped by like I always do, and she turned on me. I'm not sure what's going on with her at the moment, but she was worse than usual. She was really angry, ranting that she never got a break and how everything in life was always against her, even when she had it all planned out. Somehow, she thinks her problems are all my fault. And my dad's, of course. I just didn't feel like stopping by today."

"I'm sorry your mother hurt you like that," Shelly said. "May I suggest something, and will you think it over?"

Ashley hesitated before replying. She trusted Shelly, but if it was going to be something about patching things up with Jessica, Ashley didn't want to know. Between her mom and Jackson, she'd taken enough abuse to last a long time. "I guess," she said eventually. "It won't hurt me to hear what you have in mind."

Shelly went over to the counter and opened the till, taking out a handful of bills. "I want you to take this money. It's your pay and then some. Use it to get away for a while."

"Shell, I—"

Shelly raised her hand to stop Ashley. "Wait, I haven't finished. Call it a loan. Take some time to think about what you really want, Ash, and how you can make that happen. I'm here to help you in any way I can. If you decide you want to go to community college, you can work your shifts here around that. Please, let me help you. I can afford it. I won't go into it now, but someone helped me a long time ago, and as the saying goes, I'm paying it forward. You can do the same someday, once you get on your feet."

Ashley's eyes welled up. "Are you sure? No one's ever been this kind to me before."

Shelly's face broke into a grin. "Sure, I'm sure." She waved the money at Ashley. "Quick, take it before I change my mind. Do you have somewhere to go, and someone to take you?"

Ashley nodded. She self-consciously approached Shelly, who gave her the cash.

"Thank you," Ashley whispered, stuffing the rolled-up bills in the pocket of her jeans and taking her backpack from under the counter. She hugged Shelly who smoothed Ashley's hair and gently wiped the tears from her cheeks.

"Get out of here," Shelly said, picking up a laundry basket full of dirty clothes. "That's an order, okay?"

"I'm going," Ashley grinned, pushing past the scowling youth in the hoodie who was loitering in the doorway, and stepping into the sunlight outside.

*****

There was only one place Ashley had ever known happiness, and she didn't get to go there very often. As a child she'd spent many summers on Orcas Island, when her parents were still together, and her mother used to smile. It was the largest of the San Juan Islands and was located about a hundred miles north of Seattle. In order to get there one drove to Anacortes and then took the ferry to Eastsound on Orcas Island.

She still had fond memories of playing in the woods beside her grandparents' cabin, or on the beach until dusk with Dexter, her friend whose family lived on the island year-around. Dexter had long since moved away, but her family's cabin was still there, untouched by time. Ashley's mother had kept it after her divorce from Pat, since it was her separate property.

Ashley didn't know if her mother was aware she still visited there on occasion, the last time having been with Jackson the year before. Jackson had complained the whole time they were there about the cabin being too remote and not fitted out with modern conveniences like Wi-Fi or a smart TV set. Since watching television and playing video games were Jackson's favorite pastimes, in his opinion there was nothing to do on Orcas, and the place was beyond boring. Looking out of the window at the cars they were speeding past on Interstate 5, Ashley wished she'd dumped Jackson back then, instead of suffering another year of his slovenly ways.

"A penny for your thoughts," said the voice beside her, and she turned and smiled at the driver, her friend Sam.

"I was just thinking that what I love about Orcas is exactly what

Jackson hated. The slow pace of life, talking to people instead of being connected to devices 24/7, and being close to nature. Thanks for taking me, Sam. I really appreciate it."

Sam's freckled face beamed back at her. "I'd drive you to the end of the earth if it meant getting you away from that low-life. You've no idea how happy I was when I got your call. Are you sure you're going to be all right there by yourself, or do you want me to come across on the ferry with you?"

Ashley stared at Sam, and wished she could feel the same way about him that he seemed to feel about her. They'd first met when they were both in detention hall in high school. Ashley had forgotten her homework, and Sam had been caught skipping school to attend a band rehearsal. The rock band he formed, Meteor, went on to Billboard chart success and had even toured with Bruce Springsteen. Ginger-haired Sam was rich, charming, and had groupies throwing themselves at him, but as he often reminded her, he only had eyes for Ashley. Sometimes she caught herself wondering what it would be like to be with Sam as more than a friend, but the thought of jeopardizing their friendship had always held her back from acting on it.

"Thanks, I think I'll be fine," Ashley said. "Let's meet up when I get back." She checked herself, in case he got the wrong idea. "We can go to lunch or something."

Sam's eyes widened, and his smile grew broader, if that was possible. He began to sing the chorus of his band's latest hit. "Only got eyes for you, babe, don't you know it. If you like me too, babe, you never show it."

Ashley giggled. "Sam, you're so cheesy."

"I wrote it for you, you know that, don't you, Ashley?"

"Yeah, right. We're at Anacortes, and it looks like I'll make the next ferry crossing to Orcas. By the way, this new car of yours is pretty fast. What's it called again?"

Sam rolled his eyes. "A Porsche, Ashley, a Porsche Cayenne." He stared at her long enough for her face to flush. "I did, you know. The song, I mean. When are you going to give me a chance, Ash? How about letting me in, instead of keeping me out?"

Ashley chewed on her lower lip. Being with Sam was so easy. She hadn't thought about Jackson or her mother once since she'd left Shell's and called Sam and asked him if he could pick her up. Maybe it was time she stopped making life difficult for herself by hanging out with mean people who put her down all the time.

"Can I think it over?" she said softly. "My head's all over the place right now. I know you're one of the good guys, Sam, but I don't want to hurt you." She waved her arm up and down. "Quick, turn left at the Safeway market. The ferry terminal's down that way."

Sam checked his rearview mirror and changed lanes to make a left turn. After he'd parked at the ferry terminal, he got Ashley's backpack out of the trunk, and opened the passenger door for her. "Take all the time you need," he said, kissing her forehead when she got out. "Call me when you're ready to leave, and I'll come and get you, all right?"

Ashley nodded, and dumbly watched Sam get back in the car and drive slowly away. She waved to him, but he was too far away to see her. On the ferry, she wondered why she felt worse about Sam leaving just now than she had about Jackson leaving the night before. So many thoughts were going through her mind that she was in a world of her own on the Washington State Ferry boat trip, as well as on the taxi ride to the cabin.

"Staying long?" the taxi driver asked her as the car bumped along the potholes on the gravel road through the woods.

She realized she hadn't even thought that far ahead. "A few days, maybe longer," she said, smiling. "I'll see how it goes." Ashley wondered how long the food she'd brought with her in her backpack would last.

When she'd paid the taxi driver, and the car had turned back down the gravel road the way it had come, Ashley walked around behind the cabin to the old painted tin shed and opened the latch on the door. There was nothing of value in there, just some wood blocks and tools for the garden. She reached her hand inside the flowerpot sitting on the end of the shelf, and found what she was looking for. Her mother didn't know she kept a key hidden there, and Ashley had purposely chosen to never mention it.

The lock creaked as she turned the key to open the cabin door. She stepped into the living room and looked around. Nothing had changed since her grandparents were alive. Her mother had never updated the decor. Ashley loved the familiarity of the blanket on the sofa that her grandmother had made from knitted squares sewn together, the sheepskin rug in front of the fireplace that was yellowed with age, and the copper kettle on the stove that was blackened around the bottom. Childhood memories came flooding back, and she felt a sense of contentment settle over her as she walked across the wooden floor to the stove. When she lifted the kettle, it felt warm, which surprised her. That's when she heard the noise from the basement, a muffled banging, and what sounded like a woman yelling.

Although her heart was pounding, Ashley lifted the poker that was next to the fireplace, and started down the dark steps in the corner leading to the basement. She never noticed the baking supplies that were laid out on the dining table in the corner as she passed by it.

By the time she reached the bottom of the stairway, her hand that was holding the poker was shaking. There was definitely someone in the basement, and she quickly turned the dead bolt lock before stepping backwards. The shock on Briana's face when the door swung open was mirrored by her own.

"What on earth are you doing here?" Briana asked, as Ashley lowered the poker.

"I could ask the same of you," she said in surprise, before a sound from upstairs caused both young women to freeze.

Jessica's head appeared above them, followed by a cackling laugh. "Ashley, what good timing. I was just about to bake a cake. It's your favorite—Killer Chocolate Cake. There's plenty to go around, but I needed one more ingredient. I just got back from the store."

Jessica walked down the stairs, holding a carving knife in one hand and some nylon rope in the other hand. "But that's enough talk for now. Mommy's home, and you naughty little girls better start behaving yourselves." She stabbed the knife in the air. "Or else."

CHAPTER EIGHTEEN

"If Carlucci killed Megan and took Briana, he's gonna' regret the day he ever messed with Al De Duco's family." Al turned to Luke, who was sitting behind him on the seaplane. "Ya' never heard that, right, Luke?"

"It might not be Mario who's taken Briana. It could be Jessica Simmons," Jake pointed out.

"Ima happy to kill her too," Al muttered, before he was silenced by Cassie.

"Ssh," Cassie said. "I don't want to hear any more talk about killing anybody. As long as we get Briana home safely, that's the end of it, as far as I'm concerned. We'll leave it to law enforcement."

Luke joined the conversation. "Cassie's right, Al. It won't be necessary for you to kill anyone. I've got the local sheriff's department on standby in case we need reinforcements. I'm hoping when we find Briana it will be a quick matter of going in there and removing her from danger. If the killer is there, we'll deal with him or her in accordance with police kidnap protocol."

Al winked at Harry, who nodded toward the bag at his feet. DeeDee wondered if the bag had ever contained body parts. She tried to push the thought out of her mind, not wanting to share the ride back home with a dismembered Mario or Jessica. Meanwhile, Harry, in keeping with his librarian persona, turned back to the novel he was reading, A Tale of Two Cities by Charles Dickens. Every so often a crunching sound came from him, which was made by his teeth crushing the hard candies he popped in his mouth, one after another.

DeeDee glanced at Jake, who was sitting beside her. DeeDee, Cassie, Al, and Harry had met Jake and Luke at Lake Washington, where, thanks to Rob, a seaplane was waiting to take the six of them to Deer Harbor on Orcas Island. Rob had arranged for two cars to be waiting for them when they arrived at Deer Harbor, so they could drive to the location on the island where Briana was presumably being held captive.

Using the GPS coordinates provided by Briana's cell phone, Rob had also determined the exact location on Orcas Island where her cell phone and hopefully, Briana, were located. Also, by using the Google Maps app, he'd provided them with an aerial photograph of an old cabin that was located at the site pinpointed by the GPS.

DeeDee's stomach growled. She reached into her tote bag and pulled out a plastic container. Four heads turned when she opened it, the only exception being Harry.

"You brought cookies?" Jake asked incredulously as he reached into the container and grabbed a large circular golden cookie scattered with melted chocolate chips. He grinned. "Is it any wonder I love you?"

"I remembered I'd brought them to give to Roz," DeeDee said, passing the container around. "They're healthier than they look, and with Roz's pregnancy, she says she's eating everything in sight. Since we didn't have time for lunch, I don't think she'll mind sacrificing them to keep everyone's energy up."

Al munched a cookie. "Cassie, why can't you bake like this? Ima gonna have to divorce ya' and marry DeeDee instead."

"DeeDee's taken," Jake said. "But she can give Cassie the recipe. If you think these are good, you should try her cherry crumble. It's really something."

The trip by seaplane took about ninety minutes. DeeDee spent the time looking at the bird's eye view of Puget Sound as they traveled towards the San Juan Islands. She knew from history lessons the islands had been named after the Viceroy of Mexico who had sent an exploratory expedition to the Pacific Northwest at the end of the eighteenth century. Although DeeDee had lived in the Seattle area her whole life, she'd only visited the islands once before, on a trip with her ex-husband, Lyle. On that occasion, they'd gone to San Juan Island, which was smaller than Orcas Island, although more people lived there. She'd read somewhere that Orcas Island had a population of less than six thousand people.

After landing on the water at Deer Harbor, the seaplane taxied up to a nearby jetty. When the six passengers on the plane had disembarked, a man in a uniform bearing the logo "Orcas Rental Car" approached Al and said, "Are you Mr. De Duco?"

Al responded, "Yes, that's me. Looks like ya' gotta couple of rental cars for me, is that right?"

"Yes, sir, along with a copy of a map I was instructed by a man named Rob to give to you. He told me to tell you to just follow the map to get to where you wanted to go here on Orcas Island," the man said. "Here are the keys for the two vehicles. Hope you enjoy your stay on Orcas Island." With that the man turned and walked back to a nearby waiting car where two other rental car employees were standing.

"Cassie, DeeDee, I want you to stay with Harry," Al ordered, directing them to one of the cars. "Ima gonna' ride with Jake and Luke. Stay outta sight til' we tell ya' it's safe, okay?"

Cassie started to protest. "But Briana's my dau—"

"No buts," Al said firmly. He turned to Harry. "Ya' know the drill. Stay low unless I tell ya' otherwise. If I give the signal, we go to plan B, got it?"

Harry nodded. "Yes, Boss."

"What's plan B?" DeeDee asked.

Al lowered his voice so Luke, who was approaching the group, wouldn't hear him. "Ya' don't wanna' know. That's when me n' Harry here take care of business. Whatever it takes."

DeeDee gulped. She didn't like the sound of Plan B at all.

*****

The late afternoon sun was fading by the time the cars slowly drove through the woods toward a clearing where an old wooden cabin was visible.

"Stop here," Al said to Luke, who was driving. "There's a car parked out front. Jake, can ya' ask Rob to run a check on the license plate?"

Jake nodded. After the car stopped, Jake got out and walked down the dirt road to speak to Harry, who was driving the car behind them.

"What's happening?" Cassie asked Jake, winding down her window in the back. "Is Briana in there? I want to see my little girl."

"You have to stay here, Cassie," Jake said, his face solemn. "We don't know what we're dealing with yet. There's someone there, but we're not sure who. I'm calling Rob, so he can get more information for us."

"How will you do that, Jake?" DeeDee asked. "Cell phone service is spotty. Don't forget, we're in the middle of nowhere."

Jake pulled a radio transmitter out of his coat pocket. "I'm a private investigator. We come prepared. Sit tight, okay?"

Cassie rolled the window back up, and Jake walked into the woods, talking into the radio handset.

"The car belongs to Jessica Simmons," Jake said when he returned to where Al and Luke were waiting by the side of the first car, talking in hushed tones.

Al's face fell. "Not Carlucci? I was gonna' enjoy surprisin' him when we walked in."

Luke straightened up and pulled out his gun. "And I'm going to enjoy surprising Jessica Simmons, and holding her accountable for what she did to Megan. Are we ready, gentlemen?"

Jake and Al nodded in unison, drawing their weapons. "Let's go," Luke said.

The three men spread out as they approached the cabin, Jake and Al from either end of it, and Luke from the back. As Jake crept closer to the cabin, he could smell the unmistakable aroma of a freshly baked cake coming from an open window. Jake followed his nose, and saw Luke at the rear of the cabin. Luke's back was to the wall, his ear cocked toward the window. Jake heard the sound of twigs snapping behind him, and turned to see Al drawing closer as well. Luke raised a finger to his mouth to signal them to be quiet, and Jake and Al edged forward in silence.

Jessica's voice carried through the open window. "Just when things were going well, and I finally had a chance to make a name for myself, it all went wrong. A Gourmand Guide to Eats was an internet sensation until it's success was deliberately sabotaged. And who was to blame, huh? Your prissy, stuck-up, perfect mother, that's who."

Jake watched Al's face almost turn purple, as Al released the safety lock on his pistol. Jake frantically shook his head at Al, and held his arm out to block the back entrance of the cabin, so Al couldn't barge in and start shooting.

"That's why I'm going to kill you," Jessica continued, her voice calm and steady. Jake strained to hear what she was saying. "I tried to finish off that annoying mother of yours, but the wrong person got the special cake I made for her. Not this time, though. Oh, no. I'm going to personally feed you this delicious cake, bite by bite. The only shame is your death will be pretty quick, not as slow and painful as I'd like it to be."

"I've heard enough. I'm going in," Luke whispered. "Jake, before I storm the back, can you get up on the porch and cover me through that window? Judging by the way her voice is carrying, Jessica's up at that end."

Jake nodded while Al made a growling sound.

"Al, cover the front in case she tries to make a run for it," Luke said.

Al stomped away with a frown in his face. "Don't see why Ima missin' the action," he muttered on his way past Jake.

Jake stealthily climbed the steps on the back porch, inching his way closer to the window. He peeked around the window frame and looked inside. Jessica was standing with her back to the window, a gun trained on two women tied to chairs, their mouths taped shut. One of them was Briana, but Jake didn't recognize the other young woman. Jake could see a mortar and pestle on the countertop containing a crushed powder substance, and on the table between Jessica and the two women was a two-tier chocolate cake with a shiny chocolate glaze dripping down the sides.

Jessica was still talking. "I'll let your bodies rot in the woods. I'll let the wild critters feed off you until nothing but your bones are left. Maybe I'll post a souvenir photo for Cassie to remember you by. I think your pinkie finger would be a good one. That should be easy to chop off."

Briana, who was wriggling in the chair, her eyes wide with fear, looked up momentarily and caught sight of Jake through the window.

He ducked out of sight, holding his breath. Jessica didn't appear to have noticed.

"And you," she said, turning her gaze towards Ashley, as her voice got louder. "You're a sorry excuse for a daughter. Have I ever told you how much of a disappointment you've been to me, Ashley? I'm glad you showed up today, so I never have to see your pathetic ugly face again. If that loser of a boyfriend of yours had done what I paid him to do, and made sure the cake went to Cassie Roberts' table, none of this would have been necessary. You're indirectly to blame for your own downfall. That's rich, isn't it? Your disaster of a life has been one big waste of time, and you won't be missed by anyone, least of all, me."

Jake turned to Luke, who nodded at him. Jumping back up to the window, Jake waved his hands in a downward motion to Briana, who wobbled her chair to the side, hitting Ashley in the process. Both of the women's chairs crashed over to the floor. Sensing someone was behind her, Jessica swung around to where Jake was standing at the window, aimed her gun, and fired off a wild shot. The bullet missed him and shattered the window pane next to where he was standing. Jake couldn't fire at Jessica, because the two women on the floor were in his line of fire.

As he started to duck down below the window, he saw that Luke was inside the cabin and creeping up behind Jessica. She began firing wildly, and in the chaos that followed, Jake rushed along the porch to the back door and ran inside. Luke had been hit and was on the floor, and Jessica was crawling towards the front door of the cabin. Knowing Al would be waiting for her when she exited, Jake ran across to the three bodies lying on the floor of the cabin. Briana and Ashley were both writhing around, still tied to their chairs, but there was no movement from Luke.

Jake checked Luke's pulse, and then he heard him groan. Luke opened one eye. "I wasn't shot. She hit me with the kettle when she ran out of bullets," he moaned with a half-smile. "Help me up so I can arrest her for Megan's murder, will you?"

Jake pulled Luke up to his feet, then cut the ropes tying Briana and Ashley, before pulling the tape off their mouths. Briana winced as she stood up. "Ow."

Jake looked at them both for signs of gunshot wounds. "Have either of you been hit?"

Briana shook her head. "No, but my wrists are cut from the rope. Ashley, are you alright?"

Ashley nodded, wiping tears from her eyes. "Yes. This week has really sucked, huh?" She smiled at Briana, who put her arm around her friend and led her toward the wide-open door.

Jake followed the two girls out the front door, where Luke had arrested Jessica for the murder of Megan Reilly and was reading her the Miranda Rights.

Al was standing with a giant grin on his face, and when Cassie caught sight of Briana, she raced across the patchy grass to greet her daughter and smother her with kisses. DeeDee ran to help Ashley, and make sure she was in one piece.

Using Jake's radio transmitter, Luke called the local sheriff's office and within five minutes, they were on the scene. The paramedics put Jessica on a gurney and put her in an ambulance. Rubbing his head, Luke approached Al where he was standing beside Jake near the rental cars.

"I was wondering why you're looking so pleased with yourself, Al," Luke said. "It wouldn't have anything to do with the fact that Jessica's been shot in both legs, would it? I'm pretty sure I got her in the left leg before she crawled away, but I only shot her once."

Al stroked his chin. "I can explain that," he said. "It was self-defense. She came out waving a gun at me. What's a guy to do?" he asked.

Luke frowned. "She was out of ammo, Al. She sprayed the cabin with so many bullets, the walls look like Swiss cheese."

Al shrugged. "Well, then I guess we all had a lucky escape. C'mon, lma hungry. Where's a guy get a good steak around here, that's what I'd like to know?" He cocked his head. "Let's go."

EPILOGUE

TWO WEEKS LATER

When DeeDee, Jake and Balto arrived at Cassie and Al's new home on Bainbridge Island, the party was in full swing. Cassie met them at the door. "DeeDee! Happy birthday. That dress is beautiful."

DeeDee's face lit up, and she smiled at Jake, who was holding her hand. His blue-eyes were gazing down at her with pride. "Jake bought it for me as a surprise. He saw me admire it the evening of your birthday, when we were on the way to Le Bijou Bistro."

Cassie's forehead crinkled. "I don't think I'll ever forget that night. Come on in, everyone's waiting for you. I hope you don't mind us having our housewarming bash on your birthday, but a little birdie told me you won't be able to stay very long."

They followed Cassie down the hallway to the great room at the back of the house, where folding doors were opened onto the sprawling garden. At the end of the garden, where the grass met the water, was a small sailboat with a pink and yellow sail tied to the dock.

"That's right," DeeDee said. "We're on our way to the airport. The flight to Paris leaves at 10:35 tonight, then we transfer to Marseille, and we'll be in Provence. Thanks for watching Balto while we're away. I'm not sure who's more excited about our trip, me, or Balto, since he gets to stay with his hero, Al."

Balto wagged his tail, and raced across the grass to where Al was standing by the barbeque.

Cassie handed them both a glass of champagne. "Al's happy to have Balto here too. He knows how much Balto likes boat rides. We can all go out in our new boat." She pointed toward the sailboat on the water. "Isn't it cute? Al can't wait to start taking sailing lessons. We're going to do them together."

DeeDee sipped her champagne. "Balto will be beside himself. He won't want to come home when we get back in a week. But I thought Al wasn't a real fan of water?"

Cassie laughed. "He wasn't, but he agreed to go for some hypnotherapy treatments with a friend of mine who's a therapist, and now he's a convert. I'm telling you, I can't get him out of the pool. He's had heaters installed, and he's swimming in it twice a day."

DeeDee giggled. "That's amazing."

Al spotted them and waved. "Hey, you guys. I'm keeping the best steak for you, DeeDee, but Balto's got his eye on it, too."

"In that case, I'll be right there, Al." DeeDee looked around at the other guests milling on the lawn. "Is that Luke I see, talking to Briana?"

Cassie smiled. "Yes, the two of them have been spending time together since Luke rescued her at the cabin. He's still grieving for Megan, but they seem to have formed some type of a connection."

"I can tell where this conversation is going," Jake said, squeezing DeeDee's arm. "I'm going to go help Al with the barbecue."

DeeDee watched him walk over to Al, who greeted him with a slap on the back before swapping Jake's champagne glass for a bottle of beer. "What about Ashley?" she asked Cassie.

"She's here somewhere," Cassie said, looking around, "with a nice young man called Sam. Ash says they're not dating, but if they're not now, I'd bet they will be in the very near future. Briana told me Ashley has gotten in touch with her father, Pat, and he's going to pay for her to go to catering school. Her mother had always kept them apart, but Pat very much wants to be a part of her life."

"I'm so glad that worked out," DeeDee said. "Have you decided whether to stay on at The Seattle Times, now that Jessica's behind bars?"

Cassie's eyes twinkled. "I think so, for now. It's not exactly hard work, and I enjoy it. Al likes it too, since it gives us an excuse for date nights twice a week. Oh, I meant to ask you. How's Roz?"

"She's showing already. She and Clark are so excited about the twins. I have to say, I am too. I'm not sure Jake's so taken with the idea of us babysitting two little ones, though."

"He'll come around," Cassie said. "Let's go get some food before you guys leave for SeaTac."

As they walked across the grass, another thought occurred to DeeDee. "Did Al ever find out what the story was with Mario Carlucci? He seemed convinced Mario was out to get him."

"Apparently, Mario had other things on his mind. After we got back from Orcas Island, Al spoke to a contact of his who told him Mario got caught up with a business deal the week Megan died. If he had thoughts of causing trouble for Al and me, the dollar signs involved in the business deal got the better of him. He backed away and had nothing to do with Megan's death."

DeeDee stepped up beside Al. "Mm, that smells good. I didn't know you could cook, Al."

"There's plenty of things y'all still don't know about me," Al said with a wink. He handed her a plate with a juicy steak on it. "Here ya' go, birthday girl. The salads are over on the table. Oh, and DeeDee?"

"Yes, Al?"

"There's chocolate cake for dessert."

RECIPES

HEIRLOOM TOMATO SALAD WITH MUSTARD DRESSING & CANDIED WALNUTS

Ingredients:
4 large heirloom tomatoes
1 cup salad greens of your choice
Dressing Ingredients:
2 tbsp. red wine vinegar
1 tsp. Dijon mustard
1 tsp. salt
1 tsp. sugar
½ tsp. black pepper
½ cup extra-virgin olive oil
Candied Walnuts Ingredients:
16 oz. walnut halves
1 egg white
½ cup brown sugar, packed

Directions:
Preheat oven to 350 degrees. Lightly oil the bottom of a cookie sheet.

In a medium bowl, with a hand mixer, beat the egg white until foamy. Add the walnuts and the brown sugar. Combine until the walnuts are evenly coated. Arrange the walnuts on the baking sheet in a single layer. Bake 12-14 minutes or until golden brown. Remove from pan and cool.

Salad Dressing:
Whisk all the ingredients together until thoroughly blended. Put in refrigerator for at least one hour. (Salad dressing will keep in refrigerator for a month.)

Assembly:
Place an equal amount of the greens on four salad plates. Slice the tomatoes and arrange on the plates. Put 2-3 tablespoons of the dressing over the greens and tomatoes, per plate, depending on how much dressing you prefer. Put the unused dressing in refrigerator for another time. Scatter the walnuts over the salad. Enjoy!

NOTE: I recently made the candied walnuts and only had about 4 oz. of walnuts. The result was small cookies, which were absolutely fabulous. If you like cookies, this is really easy and wonderful!

ASPARAGUS WITH LEMON MUSTARD SAUCE

Ingredients:
1 lb. asparagus, trimmed
¼ cup plus 1 tbsp. olive oil
3 tbsp. lemon juice
1 tsp. Dijon mustard
Sea salt and freshly ground black pepper to taste

Directions:
Brush the asparagus with 1 teaspoon olive oil and season with salt to taste. Place in large frying pan and lightly cook over medium heat, turning several times, until the asparagus is tender, about 8 to 10 minutes.

While asparagus is cooking, whisk the remaining olive oil, lemon juice, and mustard in a small bowl. Season to taste with salt and pepper. Place asparagus on a serving plate and drizzle the olive oil mixture over it. Enjoy!

MAPLE GLAZED DUCK BREAST

Ingredients:
4 duck breasts, each about 8 oz.
3 tbsp. maple syrup
1 tbsp. butter
2 tbsp. brown sugar
Sea salt and freshly ground pepper to taste

Directions:
Preheat a frying pan over medium high heat. With a sharp knife, score the skin of on each duck breast in a diamond pattern, cutting through the skin and fat layer, but leaving the meat intact.

Combine the butter, maple syrup, and brown sugar in a small bowl.

Cook the duck breasts in the frying pan, skin side down, for 7 minutes. Turn the breasts over and cook them for an additional 3-5 minutes or until a thermometer reads 135 degrees. Season with salt and pepper. Enjoy!

MERINGUES

Ingredients:
4 egg whites, room temperature
½ tsp. cream of tartar or 1 tsp. lemon juice
1 cup sugar
Parchment paper
Vanilla ice cream
Chocolate Sauce
2 tbsp. slivered almonds, toasted

Directions:
Preheat oven to 225 degrees. Line a cookie sheet with parchment.

Put egg whites and the cream of tartar in a mixing bowl and beat with a mixer until foamy. Slowly add the sugar and beat until glossy and stiff. Spoon the mixture onto the parchment-lined cookie sheets, making circles approximately 4" in diameter. Place in oven for 1 1/2 hours, then turn the oven off and leave them in the oven for an additional 30 minutes.

To serve, put a scoop of vanilla ice cream on a meringue, drizzle with chocolate sauce, and scatter slivered toasted almonds on top. Makes about 12 meringues. Enjoy!

NOTE: Avoid making meringues on high humidity days. The humidity affects the sugar and makes it very difficult to get the meringue mixture stiff when you're beating it. It can also affect the meringues after they're baked, by making them soggy.

CHERRY CRUMBLE

Ingredients:
6 tbsp. butter
1 1/8 cup flour (I use rye or all-purpose white)
½ cup rolled oats
6 tbsp. packed brown sugar
1/8 tsp. salt
1 can cherry pie filling (21 oz.)
Optional: vanilla ice cream

Directions:
Preheat oven to 375 degrees. Melt butter in large saucepan. Remove from heat and stir in oats, flour, brown sugar, and salt until a crumbly dough forms. Press about 2/3 of the dough into the bottom of a 9" glass pie plate.

Spread the cherry pie filling over the oat mixture and sprinkle with the remaining oat mixture. Bake for 40-45 minutes until the top is lightly browned. Cut into desired sized pieces, top with ice cream if desired, and enjoy!

Paperbacks & Ebooks for FREE

Go to www.dianneharman.com/freepaperback.html and get your FREE copies of Dianne's books and favorite recipes immediately by signing up for her newsletter.

Once you've signed up for her newsletter you're eligible to win three paperbacks. One lucky winner is picked every week. Hurry before the offer ends!

ABOUT THE AUTHOR

Dianne lives in Huntington Beach, California, with her husband, Tom, a former California State Senator, and her boxer dog, Kelly. Her passions are cooking, reading, and dogs, so whenever she has a little free time, you can either find her in the kitchen, playing with Kelly in the back yard, or curled up with the latest book she's reading.

Her award winning books include:

Cedar Bay Cozy Mystery Series
Kelly's Koffee Shop, Murder at Jade Cove, White Cloud Retreat, Marriage and Murder, Murder in the Pearl District, Murder in Calico Gold, Murder at the Cooking School, Murder in Cuba, Trouble at the Kennel, Murder on the East Coast, Trouble at the Animal Shelter, Murder & The Movie Star, Murdered by Wine

Cedar Bay Cozy Mystery Series - Boxed Set
Cedar Bay Cozy Mysteries 1 (Books 1 to 3)
Cedar Bay Cozy Mysteries 2 (Books 4 to 6)
Cedar Bay Cozy Mysteries 3 (Books 7 to 10)
Cedar Bay Cozy Mysteries 4 (Books 11 to 13)
Cedar Bay Super Series (Books 1 to 6)... good deal
Cedar Bay Uber Series (Books 1 to 9)... great deal

Liz Lucas Cozy Mystery Series
Murder in Cottage #6, Murder & Brandy Boy, The Death Card, Murder at The Bed & Breakfast, The Blue Butterfly, Murder at the Big T Lodge, Murder in Calistoga, Murder in San Francisco

Liz Lucas Cozy Mystery Series - Boxed Set
Liz Lucas Cozy Mysteries 1 (Books 1 to 3)
Liz Lucas Cozy Mysteries 2 (Books 4 to 6)
Liz Lucas Super Series (Books 1 to 6)... good deal

High Desert Cozy Mystery Series
Murder & The Monkey Band, Murder & The Secret Cave, Murdered by Country Music, Murder at the Polo Club, Murdered by Plastic Surgery

High Desert Cozy Mystery Series - Boxed Set
High Desert Cozy Mysteries 1 (Books 1 to 3)

Northwest Cozy Mystery Series
Murder on Bainbridge Island, Murder in Whistler, Murder in Seattle, Murder after Midnight, Murder at Le Bijou Bistro

Northwest Cozy Mystery Series - Boxed Set
Northwest Cozy Mysteries 1 (Books 1 to 3)

Midwest Cozy Mystery Series
Murdered by Words, Murder at the Clinic

Jack Trout Cozy Mystery Series
Murdered in Argentina

Coyote Series
Blue Coyote Motel, Coyote in Provence, Cornered Coyote

Midlife Journey Series
Alexis

Newsletter

If you would like to be notified of her latest releases please go to www.dianneharman.com and sign up for her newsletter.

Website: www.dianneharman.com,
Blog: www.dianneharman.com/blog
Email: dianne@dianneharman.com

SURPRISE!

NEW BOOK BY B.R. SNOW - The Case of the Nattie Newfie

If you read my newsletter, you know I'm a huge fan of B.R. Snow and his brilliant series, Thousand Island Doggy Inn Mysteries. If you've ever read his books, trust me, you're in for a treat!

As the launch date of their new dog toy company approaches, Suzy, Josie, and Chef Claire are in Ottawa to do a photo shoot with their dogs as part of the initial marketing campaign. But the photographer, who moonlights for the tabloids, is a young man with a very bad public image and a reputation for being a bit of ladies' man. And when his assistant is found dead in his downtown loft, the photographer is the number one suspect. ·

Suzy soon finds herself working with two Canadian detectives she met the last time she was in town and right in the middle of a bizarre case that includes some rather scandalous photographs, blackmail, and, quite possibly, a case of mistaken identity. Further complicating things is a huge early winter snowstorm that has everyone on edge and more than a few people severely under the weather.

As Suzy digs into the case, she comes face to face with a diverse group of potential suspects including The Black Widow, a socialite with five dead ex-husbands, a mining magnate who has inexplicably signed up to be husband number six, a couple of famous models, and the aunt of Suzy's new boyfriend, Max, whose career ended abruptly when she was caught in an embarrassing situation, quite possibly by the very same photographer they're using for the dogs' photo shoot. Despite her latest resolution to take a step back and let the police do their thing, Suzy's neurons are soon on fire, and, once again, she finds herself up to her neck in the case, and up to her waist in snow before she can get a good handle on exactly what's going on.

The Case of the Natty Newfie is the latest installment in B.R. Snow's popular Thousand Islands Doggy Inn Mysteries and deals with dogs, food, and the power of friendship set in one of the most beautiful spots on the planet.

Open your smartphone, point and shoot at the QR code below. You will be taken to Amazon where you can download and read the book.

Made in the USA
Middletown, DE
08 August 2022

70851360R00097